a child for sale

BOOKS BY PAM HOWES

PAM HOWES

a child
for sale

bookouture

Published by Bookouture in 2023

An imprint of Storyfire Ltd.
Carmelite House
50 Victoria Embankment
London EC4Y 0DZ

www.bookouture.com

ISBN: 978-1-80019-792-3
eBook ISBN: 978-1-80019-791-6

This book is a work of fiction. Names, characters, businesses, organizations, places and events other than those clearly in the public domain, are either the product of the author's imagination or are used fictitiously. Any resemblance to actual persons, living or dead, events or locales is entirely coincidental.

ONE

BOLLINGTON, CHESHIRE

May 2015

Ernie Thorpe adjusted his old straw trilby over thinning grey hair, wiped his sweaty brow on the sleeve of his red-and-white-checked cotton shirt and took a long swig of water from a plastic bottle. He screwed up his face at its unexpected warmth, but he was so thirsty, he drank some nevertheless and then spat the final mouthful onto the grass.

It was a hot day alright; no wonder the water was almost undrinkable. There was little shade anywhere as the sun beat down relentlessly from a cloudless blue sky. The whole week had been unusually warm for early May; but, still, he wasn't complaining. Better than rain any day, and, as the boss wanted the whole of the front of this red-brick retaining wall cleared of clinging weeds by teatime, he'd best get a move on.

The builders would be in tomorrow to repoint the wall before they began digging the footings for a new kitchen extension. It was beyond Ernie to understand why anyone would want to build an extension on such a large house as The Pines. The original kitchen was already a good size and, in his humble opinion, it just needed a bit of a general refurbishment. But there were major plans already drawn up to turn the house into one of those fancy care homes for dementia patients and to fit it out to resemble a 1950s seaside boarding house. The idea behind it was to help enable the patients to relive their memories of past holidays. A retro but state-of-the-art kitchen was essential, so he'd been informed by the builder. The old kitchen area would then be converted into a laundry room.

Ernie had seen some changes at The Pines on leafy Dumbah Lane over the seventy-plus years he'd lived in the small Cheshire country town of Bollington. Not all of them were favourable changes either. During his childhood and teens, the house had been a private home for unmarried mothers. Run by nuns and financed partly by the Catholic Church, the home was closed down by the local authorities in the early seventies, after an unusual number of babies were reported to have died during, or shortly after, birth. He didn't know the full story. He'd always been sent out of the room to mutters of *little pigs have big ears*, whenever his mother and his aunties were gossiping in the kitchen over a pot of tea and home-made cakes.

A few years after the closure, the old house had been bought by a couple who were in the music business, recording and managing solo singers and pop groups. They'd lived here with their young daughter until ten years ago, when the husband died by suicide after being sued by angry musicians who had been swindled out of their performing and song-writing royalties. Following his death, the house was re-possessed by the bank and his penniless widow and daughter had reportedly left the UK to live in Switzerland.

The Pines had remained unsold and empty until Travellers claimed squatters' rights for a time and then nearly two years ago, the house had been sold at auction. It was purchased by a company who ran a number of care homes for vulnerable adults, in quiet countryside locations. The clientele were mainly elderly Dementia and Alzheimer's patients.

Over the last few months, Ernie had kept an interested eye on the place, observing as it had been gutted and skip after skip of rubble had been cleared away until just the bare brick walls and skeletons of the many rooms were left standing. Slowly, but surely, the developers had transformed the building, and, apart from the new kitchen still to be completed and the addition of a sunroom/conservatory at the back, it was almost finished.

Ernie was retired, but he'd run his own successful gardening business since leaving school and he still liked to keep his hand in. He now looked after just a few local gardens to help eke out his pension. One afternoon, a few weeks earlier, one of the chief contractors had been visiting his beloved elderly aunt on the other side of the village while Ernie was doing her garden. He'd been introduced to Joe Shaw as Aunty Maude's gardening angel.

On the strength of that introduction, Ernie had promptly been offered the job of part-time gardener, with the opportunity to take on the maintenance of the grounds once the building works and major landscaping had all been completed. Ernie had agreed to help, for now, but told Joe he would have to see how his back held out before he could commit himself to a full-time gardening position again. He suffered from disc problems these days; and it was one thing mowing an already neat lawn, digging out a few weeds and trimming back the odd wayward bush, but he wasn't too sure he was up to managing over an acre's worth of garden.

Anyway, there was time enough to think about that side of things. For now, he'd get this afternoon's work out of the way and look forward to going home for his tea. His wife Iris, in his opinion the best cook for miles, had promised a steak and ale pie tonight, with her special buttery mash, accompanied by peas and carrots from their own cottage garden.

He set to with a smile and stuck his fork into the ground. The force of hitting something solid jarred his shoulder and nearly sent him flying backwards into the hedge. 'What the bloody hell?' he muttered, dropping slowly to his knees to take a closer look. He scrabbled at the ground with his old gardening gloves, revealing a couple of red bricks buried in the earth. He loosened the soil around them, pulled the bricks out and tossed them into the nearby barrow. Similar bricks to the ones The Pines was built from, must have been mislaid by the original builders donkey's years ago, he thought. A bit more scrabbling and he uncovered what appeared to be a rusty-looking tin box.

He frowned. *Buried treasure? No, surely not...* Ernie loosened the earth from around the box, which was the size of a shoebox. He carefully lifted it from the hole and laid it on the grass beside him. The lid had a hinge to one long side but no locks, so it probably wouldn't contain anything of much value. If anyone was going to bury jewellery or money it would be locked. He tried to prise the lid open, but the rust was making it stick to the rim of the box. He pulled a bunch of keys from his trouser pocket and found his penknife. He ran the blade's tip round the underside of the lid edge. That seemed to help and slowly, he wriggled the box open and flipped the lid over.

He peered into the box and saw what looked like white linen, or maybe bandage fabric, tucked in all round the edges. He lifted the covering at one end and slowly pulled it back. His eyes widened with shock as he uncovered a tiny skull and what looked like ribs and other small bones. He gasped and covered the bones over again and got slowly to his feet. He felt sick.

Was this the remains of one of those dead babies he'd heard spoken about in his mother's kitchen all those years ago? What the heck should he do now? If it *was* a baby and it had been buried illegally – or even legally – then there might be others, and they'd need to be carefully removed from this makeshift graveyard and re-buried somewhere more suitable so the remains could rest in peace. Oh God, otherwise there'd be bones all over the place once the landscape gardener and his men got to work with their rotavators in the next few weeks. He'd need to stop that happening immediately. Realising his thoughts were racing, Ernie tried to take a deep breath. He was shaking. He felt even more sick, thinking of what might have happened to the poor little mites.

He took his mobile phone from his trouser pocket, mentally thanking his grandson Calvin, who'd insisted both Ernie and his Granny Iris carry them when they were out and about in case of emergencies. He briefly imagined how he'd feel if they'd lost one of their grandchildren to this place. It was too much to take in. He dialled 999 and held his breath for a moment.

'Emergency, which services do you require?' a pleasant female voice enquired.

'Oh, err, yes, police, please, I think,' he stuttered, feeling like he was about to pass out. When a police officer answered, Ernie said, 'I, erm, I'm sorry to bother you, Miss, and I'm not really certain, but I think I may have found the remains of an infant – well, I've found tiny bones and a skull in a tin box anyway.'

He realised he was gabbling as a gasp sounded at the other end of the line and the call handler quickly took his details and the address of The Pines and reassured him that someone would be with him very soon.

'Best not to touch anything else before the police arrive, sir,' she advised. 'The fewer disturbances of the area there are for the moment, the better. You just sit tight, we'll be there as soon as we can.'

TWO

WEST DERBY, LIVERPOOL

May 2015

Laura and Peter Maxwell waved goodbye as the final members of their growing family piled into the estate car and drove away from the couple's home in West Derby village.

'Phew,' Laura said, letting out a deep breath, as Pete closed the front door. They laughed together as they made their way into the lounge at the back of the house. Laura surveyed the untidy scene and shook her head. There were toys and books everywhere. 'I suppose I'd better start to tidy up.'

'Leave it for now, love. Sit down and let's have a quiet drink together,' Pete suggested, clearing a collection of furry teddies off the sofa. 'It can wait. We've got all day tomorrow to clear up. We deserve a little rest now. Much as we love them, there's always a feeling of relief as they leave,' he admitted with a sheepish grin.

Laura laughed. 'Go on then,' she said. 'I'll have a G&T, please, not too large and no ice.' She sat down in the space Pete had cleared and kicked off her strappy silver sandals. She looked across to the fire surround at her lovely birthday cards standing on the mantle and smiled. Vases of colourful summer flowers adorned the sideboard under the window, and boxes of chocolates, alongside her favourite toiletries and some gift vouchers, sat on the side table next to the sofa. As always, her lovely and thoughtful family had done her proud.

Her two married daughters and their husbands, along with six assorted grandchildren, three in each family, had been for a buffet tea to celebrate Laura's sixty-eighth birthday. As usually happened when the whole crew were here, it grew slightly chaotic as the evening wore on. The two girls talked incessantly, as though they hadn't seen each other for years, even though they lived within a mile of each other and met a couple of times a week at least. The menfolk talked football and snooker and the younger kids fell out over the games and toys as they became tired and a bit fractious. Both she and Pete loved having them all round, but it was also nice to get the house back to themselves at the end of the visit.

She smiled as Pete came back into the lounge carrying two glasses and handed one to her. 'Thanks, love.'

Pete sat down next to her, looked at his watch and reached for the TV remote on the coffee table, pressing the on switch. 'News is on in five minutes,' he announced, taking a sip of his drink. He clinked his glass against hers. 'Happy birthday again, my love. Have you enjoyed yourself, in spite of the racket?'

She nodded. 'I certainly have,' she said. 'We're used to such a quiet life since we retired that it's hard at times when they all descend at once. But I wouldn't have it any other way. You know that, don't you?'

He smiled and reached for her hand. 'I do. And nor would I.' He looked to the TV screen as the ITV news programme started. 'I wonder what joys we are in for tonight?' he said, rolling his eyes. 'More political shenanigans, I suppose, while the country adjusts to a Tory government.'

'No doubt,' Laura agreed with a sigh. Every night this week

it had been the same old, same old. Her favourite soaps and drama programmes had been shunted around while party political debates went on and on. David Cameron had just succeeded Gordon Brown at Number 10 Downing Street. One thing Laura couldn't stand was politics. No matter who was in at Number 10, not much ever changed for pensioners like her and Pete. 'But while you shout at the telly, I'm popping to the bathroom, and I'll get ready for bed while I'm up there.'

'Right you are,' he said as she put down her empty glass and stood up. 'I'll have a refill ready and waiting for when you come back down.'

'Are you trying to get me tipsy for some reason, Peter Maxwell?' She picked up her discarded sandals and raised an eyebrow.

'Moi?' he said, his blue eyes twinkling with amusement. 'Now why would I do that?' He grinned as she shook her head and left the room.

Upstairs, Laura looked out of the landing window at the bright crescent moon that hung between the two houses bordering their large back garden. It was a clear night and the sky was full of stars. Even the moon had a huge bright star sitting just above its uppermost curve. After such a lovely day, it felt like the stunning display was just for her.

Maybe it was a planet, Jupiter or Mars, she had no idea which. Their eldest grandson Julian would know though. He was really good at all things to do with astronomy. *He'll go far, that one*, she thought proudly. Julian was their eldest daughter Rosie's only son. The family was convinced he was destined for university, unlike his two sisters, who weren't in the least bit academic.

She smiled as she strolled into the bathroom. Her granddaughters were fashion and music mad, both crazy about Harry

Styles from the boy band One Direction. Typical young teenage girls really, just like she herself had been at their ages, except her idol had been Beatle Paul McCartney. Their six grandchildren ranged from Julian at nearly sixteen, down to three-year-old Marcus, who belonged to their youngest daughter Penny. They certainly kept the family busy; she and Pete helped with childminding when they could.

In the bedroom she drew the curtains, put her sandals on the shoe rack and took off her best red dress that she'd worn for the party. She loved the colour and knew it suited her dark hair, and she'd painted her finger- and toenails in a matching red. She hung the dress on a hanger and pushed it into the over-full wardrobe. One day soon she would have that clear-out of clothes that she'd been promising herself for months.

Trouble was, there was nothing she really wanted to get rid of. She always chose her clothes carefully, and mixed and matched so that she looked as fashionable and trendy as she could without looking *like mutton dressed as lamb*, as her late mother would have said. She and her best friend Anna had often had the discussion about what age should they start shopping for 'old-lady style clothes'. Anna always said there was not a chance it would ever happen, and Laura was inclined to agree with her.

Having trendy daughters helped to keep her on her toes, and, if there eventually came a time when the family decided to shunt her and Pete off into a twilight home for the totally confused, then it wouldn't matter what they wore as the clothes would be chosen for them by carers and the choice would be out of their hands. But for now, Laura would continue to wear what she knew suited her best.

She wore her slim-fitting jeans and nice tops for everyday, with a stylish leather or denim jacket, and Pete was always more comfortable in his jeans and a smart leather jacket than formal wear. They were a well-matched pair, she thought, but then they always had been, right since their mid-teens when they first met at St Bernadette's youth club in their hometown, which was near Manchester, and began dating. They'd fallen in love almost immediately and had been so happy, until...

Laura took a deep breath and blinked rapidly before the tears started. If they took hold, she wouldn't be able to stop. She hadn't been expecting to think about that time today, but it could still catch up with her, even after all these years. She shook her head to clear the long-ago memories, sat down in front of the dressing table mirror and carefully removed her make-up with Anne French cleansing milk. She wiped her face with Liz Earle toner and then smoothed on Oil of Olay moisturiser, dabbing carefully under her blue eyes. She smiled as she fastened the top back on the bottle.

When she first started to use the product, it was called Oil of Ulay, but Anna, who had relatives in Canada and often went to visit, had told her it was named Olay over there and the UK were the only country to call it Ulay. Laura supposed it was a case of catching up with the rest of the world. Whatever, it kept the wrinkles under control and that was the main thing. She unpinned her dark-brown hair and let it fall to her shoulders, running her fingers through the length to smooth out the tangles, pleased her roots were showing no stray greys since her visit to the hairdresser's the other day.

Honestly, it was a work of art to keep the years at bay nowadays. It was so much easier for men as they aged. Pete's hair was silver all over now, but it suited him. She called him her silver fox and it made him laugh. As she reached into the dressing table drawer for a pair of cotton pyjamas she could hear his voice rising, and realised he wasn't shouting at the telly about the political news, but urgently calling out her name. Hurriedly checking her eyes weren't too puffy, she pulled on her pyjamas, pushed her feet into slippers and dashed onto the landing.

He was standing at the bottom of the stairs, looking anxious and beckoning for her to hurry down.

'What is it?' she asked as she joined him in the hall.

He pointed to the sitting room door, his hand shaking slightly. '*Granada Reports* is about to start and they just ran through the headlines like they always do. Go and sit down, quick. We need to watch this; it's the second item they mentioned, it'll be on next.'

Laura nodded and sat down on the sofa, wondering what he was talking about. True to his earlier word, Pete had refilled her glass, and she took it as he handed it to her. She looked at him as he sat down beside her and chewed his lip agitatedly while they waited for the newsreader to finish a report about local council updates and their elected candidates.

'Now,' Pete said and pointed at the screen as a large house came into view, with a police presence and what looked like the striped tape they used to cordon off an area where a crime had been committed.

Laura's eyes opened wide as the reporter looked at the camera with a serious expression on his face. He began to speak, explaining that he was in a Cheshire village outside a private property that was in the throes of being renovated. He went on to say that the large garden had been taped off to prevent anyone trespassing while a search was ongoing.

'A number of bones were discovered earlier today, buried in the garden in a box. They are believed to be the remains of an infant, and, while foul play isn't suspected at this moment, a search is now on to investigate and to look for further possible remains. The house has had several uses over the past decades and in the late fifties and early to mid-sixties was a home for unmarried mothers. The home was closed down and the property was badly damaged by fire a few years ago. We will bring you an update as soon as we have any further details.'

Laura took a deep breath as Pete grasped her hand. Tears

rolled down her cheeks and he put his arms round her and held her tight.

'It's definitely The Pines, isn't it?' she whispered. 'I thought I'd never see that place again.' She sobbed into Pete's chest.

'I know,' he whispered back. 'Me neither. Whoever's baby it was, its resting place has been disturbed. The poor little soul; I wonder how many more they'll find.'

Laura slowly sat up and shook her head. 'There were at least four babies born dead that we were told were buried in the garden in the few months I was there. Oh God, Pete! Anna's daughters were buried in that garden. I wonder if she's seen the news.' As she spoke, the phone rang out in the hallway and Pete hurried to answer it.

'It's Anna,' he called, handing the phone to Laura as she dashed to his side. He sat down on the stairs as Laura took the receiver from him.

As she finished her conversation, Pete heard Laura agreeing that Anna and her husband Mick should come over in the morning. She said goodbye and replaced the phone on its cradle.

'They've just seen the news and of course Anna recognised the house right away. But they've both had a drink, so they won't drive over tonight.' Laura took a deep shuddering breath. 'Anna's distraught. She's convinced they've disturbed one of her twins' graves.'

Pete nodded. 'I bet she is. But it could be any of the poor little babies that didn't make it. They're going to have to try and exhume as many as they can and maybe re-bury them in the village churchyard. I can't understand why that wasn't done in the first place. Surely it's unlawful to bury babies in a bloody garden anyway.'

Laura shrugged her shoulders. 'Who knows? Those nuns

were a law unto themselves and we didn't dare question them. Oh, Pete, this is going to bring back all those awful sad memories of our Paul that I try and keep in the back of my mind.' She burst into tears and Pete held her in his arms, his own tears mingling with hers.

THREE

DIDSBURY, MANCHESTER

June 1964

Laura Sims jumped off the bus and let herself into the smart semi-detached house on Parrs Wood Road, where she lived with her recently widowed mother, Audrey. The house was silent, meaning Mum, and her sister, Laura's Aunty Lillian, who seemed to spend more time here than in her own home since Dad had passed away just before last Christmas, were hopefully still out at one of their endless women's group meetings down at the church hall.

She hung her jacket over the end of the newel post and placed her briefcase on the bottom stair ready to take up to her bedroom later. In the kitchen, she filled the kettle and placed it on the gas hob. Normally, after college, she'd go for a frothy coffee with a few of her friends in one of the coffee bars in Didsbury village, but today, she just felt really tired and weary and needed a bit of a rest before she tackled her art project homework. Then she'd need to get ready to meet her boyfriend Pete for a night of music and dancing at nearby St Bernadette's youth club.

She made a half-pot of tea and waited while it brewed before pouring a mug, taking care to use the tea strainer as floating tea leaves always turned her stomach. Her mum wouldn't hear of trying the new tea bags that were becoming popular. *Too expensive*, she said. But it would save having a mouthful of yucky tea leaves at the bottom of a mug if she'd only give them a try. Maybe some more sugar would perk her up a bit, Laura thought, and added an extra spoonful. That should give her a spurt of energy and at least keep her awake for a while longer so she could tackle some of her project.

She rooted in the biscuit barrel for a couple of custard creams and took her snack upstairs. Her pet cat Sooty was stretched out on the pink candlewick bedspread, and he rolled over and stretched as she walked into the room and put her plate on the bedside table. 'You'll be in trouble if Mum sees you on the bed,' she warned him, and hurried back down the stairs to pick up her briefcase.

She dropped it on the bedroom floor and sat on her bed with her back against the pink padded headboard and floral pillows to enjoy her brew and biscuits. Mum didn't like Sooty to get on the beds in case he had fleas. But he seemed clean enough to Laura; his short black coat was glossy and smooth and he hardly ever scratched either. Scratching was a sure sign of fleas, her mum reckoned.

Sooty stretched out beside her and she tickled his ears and stroked the top of his head. He purred loudly, and ecstatically kneaded the bedspread with chubby white paws that reminded Laura of little socks on each foot. Dad had brought him home from work as a tiny fluffy baby nearly eight years ago now.

Sooty was one of the kittens of a cat that lived at a station her dad passed through regularly in his job as a train driver. On a stopover one night the stationmaster had asked him if his daughter would like a kitten as he'd got some ready to leave the mother cat and was looking for new homes for them, but when he'd mentioned it to her the next day, Mum had said she wasn't having any cats in her house.

However, her objections fell on deaf ears and Sooty came home in the khaki green canvas bag Dad took his dinnertime sandwiches in. Winking at Laura, who remembered now how she'd squealed with delight when she caught sight of Sooty, he fibbed that the kitten must have climbed in while his bag was on the floor in the station canteen and that it would be cruel to take him back, especially now that Laura had seen him.

She smiled now and tickled his belly. Sooty knew all her secrets. She'd cried into his neck when Dad had his heart attack at the young age of forty-five and she'd sobbed into his fur when her father had passed away that same night in nearby Wythenshawe Hospital. The night she first met Pete she'd told Sooty all about him and how much she liked the boy who had asked her to dance when the youth club disc jockey played 'Be My Baby' by an American girl group that everyone was raving over, the Ronettes.

After each subsequent date since, Sooty had been her confidant, and of course he kept all her secrets to himself. Thank goodness he couldn't talk. Her mum didn't approve of Laura having a boyfriend, never mind that the pair of them had fallen in love very quickly. She also wasn't happy that Laura had chosen to study art at college, telling her that no good would come of an art qualification when she could be learning to type and become a secretary. *A proper job*, as she deemed it. But Laura loved going to Hollings College, known locally as the Toast Rack because of the building's unique structure. Her ambition was to design fashionable clothes, maybe even have her own business eventually. Pete was doing an apprenticeship at Fairey Aviation in Manchester. They both had decent futures to look forward to; or rather, they had, until recently. And that was something they needed to talk long and hard about when they met up tonight. Laura finished her tea and took her sketch pad from her briefcase along with her pencil case.

Half an hour later, just as she was completing a design for a simple sleeveless shift-style knee-length dress, she grimaced as she heard the front door open and her mum calling her name. 'I'm upstairs,' she called back. 'I'm just finishing some homework.' She rolled her eyes as footsteps thudded on the stairs and her mother's head, complete with her usual smart red velvet pillbox hat over carefully set mouse-brown hair, appeared round the open door.

'Get that cat off the bed,' Audrey Sims ordered, narrowing her unfriendly green eyes at Sooty before issuing a greeting to her daughter.

'He's not doing any harm,' Laura protested as Sooty flinched and jumped down at the sound of raised voices. He hissed at her mum and ran under the bed to hide.

'I've told you a million times he's not to go on the beds,' Audrey exaggerated. 'I might just as well talk to a brick wall for all the notice you take of me these days. Anyway, what do you want for your tea?' she demanded, abruptly changing the subject. 'Only I was thinking of making a cottage pie.'

Laura wrinkled her nose. Cottage pie was the last thing she felt like eating right now. 'No thanks, Mum. I'll just have some cheese on toast. I'm really not that hungry and I don't have time tonight to wait until it's cooked.'

Audrey frowned. 'It's unlike you not to be hungry. Hope you're not sickening for something. You look a bit pale. There are all sorts of bugs going round. Oh well, if you're quite sure. I'll save the minced meat until tomorrow and make it then instead.'

Laura nodded. 'I'm sure. I'll finish up here and then I'll pop down and eat and then I'll get ready to go out.'

Audrey pursed her thin lips. 'I suppose you're going out

with that lad from the Wythenshawe estate again? I hope he's not coming to the house on that motorbike to pick you up.'

Laura sighed and shook her head. 'I'm meeting him at the youth club so don't worry, I won't show you up in front of your neighbours. And it's a Lambretta scooter he rides. He's a Mod, for goodness' sake, they don't ride motorbikes.'

Audrey raised her well-plucked eyebrows. 'I don't care what he is, and a bike's a bike, no matter what fancy name you choose to give it. Why you can't pick a nice lad like the one Brenda next door is going out with, I don't know.'

Laura gritted her teeth and took a deep breath. Brenda's spotty, blond-haired boyfriend Barry was a junior bank clerk who was at least three inches shorter than Brenda was and not Laura's type at all. Pete, on the other hand, was tall and dark-haired with big blue eyes. The night they'd met he'd looked so handsome in his long black leather coat and smartly pressed Levi jeans, his hair cut in a trendy Mod style, he'd swept her off her feet immediately.

Laura loved going to his house. It was busy and noisier than she was used to, as he was the eldest of four brothers and she was an only child. The family lived in a council house on an estate that was big but friendly and everyone spoke to their neighbours and helped each other out. Folk weren't snobby like round here. Most of the well-heeled neighbours on this partic-ular end of the road thought they were a cut above everyone else, as did her mother.

That's what Laura missed about her dad. The fact that he was so down to earth in spite of his snobby wife and her equally snobby and bossy sister, who'd told him shortly before he died that it was high time he had his own station. He'd retaliated with his usual sense of humour that it was a good job he didn't as he couldn't see Audrey settling into a tiny cottage, beside a noisy railway line, as the stationmaster's wife.

Laura had often heard her parents arguing and wasn't in the

least bit surprised that Dad loved his job, which took him away overnight many times during the week. Driving his train up and down the country was probably the only time he felt he'd got any peace to just be himself. She'd loved it when he was at home and her mum was out at one of her meetings. They'd watched programmes on the telly that Mum would never agree to watching, music ones like the *Six-Five Special*, *Ready Steady Go!*, and more recently, *Top of the Pops*.

Her dad had loved music, a love he'd shared with his daughter. He'd bought her a Dansette record player the year before he died and each time she got her weekly spending money, she'd saved a bit until she could treat herself to the latest top ten singles. She had quite a collection now. She missed their special times together and was so glad she'd met Pete, who filled the awful emptiness that losing her dad had left her with.

Pete's mum and dad went regularly to a local social club on a Saturday night, and often talked about the live acts they saw and how his mum occasionally won a few bob playing bingo. With his brothers also out with their mates and girlfriends, Pete and Laura had the house to themselves. They played records and made love in the bedroom he shared with his younger brother Ross. It always felt like home.

Laura handed her jacket to the cloakroom checkout girl, smoothed down the skirt of her black-and-white minidress and made her way into the large church hall where the youth club was held. The room was dimly lit and a few couples were already up dancing as the regular disc jockey played a selection of popular records. She spotted Pete standing by the small soft drinks bar talking to a couple of his mates and hurried across to join him. He turned as she called his name and he held out his arms. She ran into them and he hugged her tight. 'We need to talk,' she whispered, 'privately, on our own.'

'Okay then,' he whispered back, pulling her to one side. 'Let's find a table where we can sit and talk before it gets too crowded in here. Do you want a Coke while we're at the bar?'

'Please,' she replied, casting her gaze around the room and spotting a table right at the back. 'I'll go and grab us that table back there,' she said and hurried across the room. Feeling nervous at what she was going to tell him, she pulled out a couple of chairs and sat down, quickly looking round to see if there were any of her friends in yet, but she couldn't see any of the girls from college, or her old school friends. That was good. They wouldn't be disturbed for a while at least.

Pete joined her and handed her a bottle of Coke complete with a straw. He sat down next to her and reached for her hand, his face serious as he gazed into her eyes. She smiled as he squeezed her hand tight and took a sip of his drink.

'You okay?' he asked, frowning as she shook her head.

'Not really,' she began, her voice wobbling. 'You know I told you the other day that I was late... well, today I felt a bit off colour at college and not too good at all. I really do think I might be pregnant, Pete.'

He nodded. 'I thought you might be,' he said. 'I've been thinking about what you said the other day. Don't worry, we're in this together. If you are then we need to make some plans. You know I love you, don't you? We wouldn't be in this mess if it wasn't for love.'

She nodded, feeling relieved. 'And I love you too. But I'm so scared. Mum will kill me. Well, she'll go absolutely berserk, anyway.'

'I don't think mine will be very happy either,' he said with a half-smile. 'But first, we need to make sure you definitely are. I hope you don't mind, but after you told me you were late, I confided in one of the guys I'm working with. He's married now, but he told me that when he got his girl into trouble they had a test done at Boots, the chemist in town.'

'Okay.' Laura frowned. 'What sort of a test?'

'A urine test. You have to take a sample in a small bottle to the chemist bit where they do prescriptions, pay a fee and they send it away to be tested. The results come back in a few days with a yes or a no; well, I mean a positive or a negative result. It's that big Boots chemist on Market Street. I thought maybe you could do that tomorrow if you can get a couple of hours out of college and pop down on the bus. I'll give you the money to pay for it.'

Laura nodded. 'Okay, so by this time next week we'll know one way or the other. And if I am, what then?'

'We'll tell our parents right away and then we'll get married. We'd be getting married eventually anyway.'

Laura nodded again and then smiled ruefully. 'You've got it all worked out, haven't you?'

'I've thought about nothing else,' he said. 'Trying to work out what's best. God knows where we'll live and I know they'll say we're too young, but something will turn up, I'm sure. The main thing is, we love one another, we'll make it work and we'll love our baby when it arrives too.'

FOUR

DIDSBURY, MANCHESTER

July 1964

Laura took a deep breath as she hurried down the stairs and made her way into the dining room at the back of the house. Her mother was just finishing off the ironing and folding a sheet to put on the pile of things to take upstairs.

'Would you like me to take those up for you?' Laura pointed towards the table.

Audrey frowned and shook her head. 'No, I'll do it. You'll get them creased, knowing you. Anyway, I thought you were getting ready to go out. Isn't it the youth club tonight again?'

Laura nodded. 'Err, yes, that's right, it is, but we're not going tonight.' She tried to clear her throat and carried on. 'Pete's coming over here instead and we might go for a walk later, it all depends.' Laura swallowed the nervous lump in her throat that was threatening to choke her.

Pete was coming to tell her mum that they wanted to get married. The recent pregnancy test result had been positive, so they'd made the decision to break the news to their mothers as soon as they could. Pete had told his own parents the same night the result was back and, although they'd not been happy with him, they'd told him they would help where they could when the young couple decided what they were going to do.

Pete's mum, Angie, was accompanying him later to discuss the situation with Laura and *her* mum. Laura was dreading it. Angie was lovely and friendly to her as a rule and Laura just hoped this wouldn't make any difference to how they got on. She'd always insisted Laura call her Angie instead of Mrs Maxwell. First names were not something her mum would ever approve of.

'What do you mean, he's coming here?' Audrey demanded, picking up the pile of ironing. 'You know I don't like him coming in this house. Heaven knows what the neighbours will think, seeing him turning up on that noisy motorbike and all. You'd better phone him and tell him not to bother; you'll meet him at the church hall.'

Laura glanced over at the clock on the mantle shelf above the fireplace. 'Too late, he'll have left home by now. And like I told you before, it's a scooter not a motorbike, and it isn't noisy. He'll be here very soon.'

'Well, you'd better get ready to go straight out then. I'm not having him coming in here.' Audrey stomped out of the room, her arms laden with the ironing, and hurried up the stairs.

Laura shook her head in despair. Pete and Angie would be here any minute and then God help them all. She often wondered what on earth had happened in her mother's life that had made her turn into such a miserable person. She'd been bad enough before Dad passed away, always grumbling about something or other, begrudging them any fun, but she was ten times worse now.

Her lovely dad would have stood by her, Laura thought, of that she was certain; he would have helped her no matter what her mum would have to say about things. The sound of Pete's Lambretta engine on the drive had her quaking in her shoes and feeling queasy. More so than she'd felt in the mornings for the last few weeks – at least she'd been lucky there compared to what she'd read about morning sickness in magazine articles on early pregnancy. She jumped as her mother's voice screeched from the top of the stairs.

'That boy is here on that damn bike and he's got someone with him sitting on the back. He's just pulled on to the drive. I saw them from the front bedroom window. Tell him to put it back on the road right away. I don't want any oil leaks left on my drive.'

'The scooter's not leaking oil, it's almost new. And no, Mum, I won't tell him to get off the drive. Don't be so rude,' Laura yelled back, trying to take control of the situation. 'And the person on the back is Pete's mother. She's come to see you. We all need to talk.'

'Talk?' Audrey snapped. 'What do you mean, talk? Why on earth would I have anything to say to a person like her?'

'Mum, don't be so snobby, she's a very nice lady. I'm going to let them in now, so come down and meet her, please. You've already met Pete so try and be a bit more polite to him than you were the last time he came here.' Laura took a deep breath and then flung open the door and greeted her visitors with a welcoming smile.

Pete hugged her and Angie also gave her a quick hug. 'Do you have a mirror handy, love?' she asked Laura. 'My hair must look a right ruddy mess after that journey. I should have worn a headscarf. I never gave it a thought, silly me.'

Laura pointed to a framed mirror on the hall wall and Angie took a comb from the shoulder bag that was looped across her body. 'Dear me, look at the state of me. Looks like a flippin' haystack on top of me head.' She ran her comb through the bleached-blonde tangle and then stopped and stared as Laura's mother hurried down the stairs, her face red and twisted with anger. 'Ooh, hello, Mrs, err...' Angie began.

'Sims,' Audrey replied stiffly. 'Mrs Sims.'

'Right you are, love. I'm Angie and of course you know me son here, our Peter.' Angie smiled pleasantly, seemingly unfazed by the unwelcoming atmosphere in the hallway.

Laura quickly took charge and pushed open the lounge door as her mum's eyes nearly popped out of her head. The room was only ever used on special occasions, but there were more seats in here than in the back sitting room that also served as the dining room. 'Follow me,' she announced as Angie did as she was asked, closely followed by Pete, who squeezed Laura's hand tightly.

'I'm dreading this,' she whispered.

'Me too,' he whispered back. 'Just remember that I love you.'

She nodded. 'And I love you.'

She gestured to the beige tweed armchair in the bay window for Angie to take a seat as Laura's mother marched in and sat down on the matching armchair opposite. They were like chalk and cheese, Laura thought as she and Pete sat side by side on the sofa. Any other time it would have made her giggle, but not tonight.

'So is someone going to tell me what is going on?' Audrey demanded, staring at the others in turn. 'And why you two are here uninvited in my home?'

Pete took Laura's hand and held it tight. He looked into her eyes and smiled before looking directly at her mother. 'Actually, Laura invited us, Mrs Sims. We're here because we have something important to discuss with you,' he said, squeezing Laura's hand. 'Laura and I would like to get married and, as we're both under twenty-one and need parental consent, I've come to ask your permission for her hand.'

A choking noise from the direction of her mother, followed

by an outraged bellow as Audrey got to her feet, had both Laura and Angie jumping quickly to her side.

'What did you say?' Audrey yelled as she pushed them away. 'Marry my daughter? Is this some kind of joke, young man? You will marry my girl over my dead body!'

'And it will be if you don't calm yourself down, Mrs,' Angie said. 'You've gone the colour of boiled beetroot. Let my son speak before you cut him down like that. He's a good lad, is my Peter. Hear what he has to say.'

'You're both far too young to be thinking about marriage,' Audrey protested, ignoring what Angie had said to her. 'Laura's only seventeen, and she's still at college. I want her to make something of herself first.'

Pete nodded as Audrey slumped back into the armchair, fanning her face with her hand. 'Yes, and so do I. But maybe if you let me finish?' he suggested quietly.

'I don't care what you've got to say,' Audrey said. 'You're *not* marrying my daughter and that's that. There's nothing more to discuss.' She got to her feet again. 'Now if you don't mind, I'd like you to leave my home. And you,' she aimed at Laura, 'get up to your room while I see them out. I'll deal with you later.'

Fighting back tears, Laura looked at Pete and nodded as he chewed his lip. 'Mum, please stop interrupting him. Sit back down. Carry on, Pete, please,' she begged as her mother sank slowly back into the chair, gripping the arms, her knuckles white and Laura sat down beside Pete again.

'Mrs Sims,' Pete began again, 'Laura and I love each other very much, and err, well, she is expecting my baby. I want to do the right thing by her, so will you please give her the permission to marry me. My parents have given their permission.'

Laura crossed her fingers on her lap as she stared at her mother, whose face went white and then returned to its earlier beetroot colour. Her green eyes were filled with anger and hatred as she glared at Pete and his mum. 'Mum, please say something,' she begged.

Audrey shook her head and clutched her chest. 'Get out of my house,' she snapped, spittle flying from her pinched lips. She rose to her feet and pointed to the door. 'Go, now before I call the police.'

Angie shook her head despairingly as Laura gave way to her tears and sobbed in Pete's arms.

'Call the police?' Angie exclaimed. 'And tell them what exactly? That two young people have fallen in love; that they've slipped up and want to get married? How ridiculous do you think that would sound? Get a grip for goodness' sake, you stupid woman!'

Audrey burst into angry tears. 'How dare you speak to me like that in my own home! Get out and take that disgusting boy of yours with you.' She turned to Pete and yelled, 'It's a bit too late to be doing the right thing. You shouldn't have laid a finger on Laura in the first place. Did he force himself on you?' she aimed at Laura.

'Don't you dare insinuate my son would do such a thing,' Angie cried angrily. 'He's a decent boy, been brought up proper, he has. He would never do a thing like that.'

'Brought up proper!' Audrey yelled, mimicking Angie's strong Manchester accent. 'Yes, of course he has. I mean with you as his mother he wouldn't have been brought up any other way, would he?' she finished with sarcasm.

Laura got to her feet, still sobbing. 'Mum, how could you? Pete and I love each other so much. Of course he didn't force himself on me. He'd never do that.'

'So, you consented?' Audrey turned her furious gaze on Laura, raised her hand and smacked her soundly across the face. 'You dirty little slut!'

Laura screamed and turned to Pete, who pulled her into his arms.

Angie stared open-mouthed at the furious woman and shook her head. 'What sort of a mother does that to her pregnant daughter? Have you no feelings at all? Your girl is worried and upset and all you can do is slap her in the face. That's abuse and I've a good mind to report you. I'm not sure I want my son to marry into a family like this anyway. You're not normal,' she finished as Audrey ran from the room and pounded up the stairs. 'Come on, Peter, let's get out of this bloody madhouse. Take me home, son. Your father will have something to say about this little lot, I'm sure.'

'I can't leave Laura in this state, Mum,' Pete protested as his mother walked out of the room and let herself out of the front door without saying goodbye to Laura.

Laura turned her tear-stained face to his. 'Take your mum home, Pete. You can't leave her standing outside. She's really upset and I don't blame her. I'll try and talk to mine and see if I can get her to understand, make her see sense. But after that performance I don't hold out much hope. All being well, I'll maybe see you tomorrow.'

Pete nodded slowly. 'Pack a bag tonight and I'll come for you in the morning. I can't let you stay here with her. She's crackers. We'll do something; go somewhere, maybe that Gretna Green place where we can get married under twenty-one without parental permission. I'd take you home with me now but Mum's on the pillion seat.' He paused. 'I could come back for you later though.'

Laura tearfully shook her head. 'Not tonight. It would only cause more trouble. Let me try and sort things out with Mum. I can hear her talking; she'll be on the upstairs phone to my aunty, no doubt. I'm sorry she was so awful to you both. I honestly don't know what I was expecting, but certainly not that. I won't go in to college tomorrow, and I'll be ready to go away with you in the morning. Come over after about ten o'clock. Mum's usually out with Aunty Lillian by that time. I love you, Pete, with all my heart, and I always will.'

He hugged her tight and dropped a kiss on her lips, gently stroking her cheek, which was bright red from the slap. 'My poor girl, I love you too, more than you'll ever know. I'll see you in the morning.'

FIVE

WEST DERBY, LIVERPOOL

May 2015

Laura welcomed Anna and her husband Mick into her home and took them through into the lounge. Pete brought a tray of coffee and cake through and placed it on the coffee table. The television set was switched on, and they all waited for the midday news update.

'Sit yourselves down.' Laura gestured to the sofa and Anna and Mick sank thankfully onto the soft cushions. She handed mugs of coffee to them. 'Help yourself to cake, it's left over from my birthday party yesterday. Thanks for your card and the M&S voucher, by the way. It's much appreciated.'

'You're very welcome,' Anna said. 'We *were* planning to take the pair of you down to the Albert Dock for a celebratory lunch later this week. Maybe we still can, depending on what's happening with the latest news from The Pines.'

Pete nodded. 'That would be a nice treat. Do us all good. I think we need it. Let's see if there's anything more happened since last night,' he said as the *Granada Reports* news started and they all turned their attention to the TV screen. The same reporter from last night explained that the search for further remains continued and Laura put her arm around Anna's shoulders and gave her a hug as both their eyes filled with tears.

Pete turned off the TV and shook his head. 'I actually think we should go over to Bollington and see if anyone on site there can give us some answers,' he suggested, 'Are you two free tomorrow?

'We'll get over there first thing,' he continued as Anna and Mick nodded their heads. 'We'll come and pick you up after the rush hour traffic calms down and drive over to Cheshire. We may get more information from the police on site. That reporter guy said more bones had been recovered and all the building work is suspended for the time being.'

'If both my babies have been discovered then I want to give them a proper resting place,' Anna said tearfully. 'It's the least I can do for them. My poor little girls,' she sobbed as Mick put his arms round her. 'As if we didn't go through enough when they were born, not to mention what happened to *me* afterwards. I'll never forgive my parents for what they put us through, it was totally unnecessary. I'll need to speak with Tony's mam and ask if she's seen the news about this. It will bring it all back to her, when she lost Tony and then I lost her newborn granddaughters.'

Laura fought back tears as she remembered back to the awful time in 1964 when she'd met Anna, and how the young girl had been so distraught about her boyfriend Tony's sudden death in a motorcycle accident and then finding herself pregnant shortly after his funeral and packed off by her unfeeling parents to The Pines. Laura's own so-called mother had been totally unreasonable about her pregnancy and she'd never forgiven her for sending her to The Pines against her will too. 'It was an awful time for us all,' she said, a sob catching in her throat. 'Not something we will ever forgive or forget.'

* * *

The following morning, as Pete tried to drive his car down Dumbah Lane in Bollington, he was stopped by a young policeman and asked to turn round. 'If I park up on the lane, can we approach the site on foot?' he asked. 'We have a lady here with us,' he inclined his head towards Anna, in the back of the car, 'who might be able to help with the inquiry.'

The young man's eyebrows rose and he nodded. 'You can try,' he replied. 'You're not the only ones who've turned up with information they reckon will help, so they're a bit busy at the moment.'

'I didn't think we would be,' Pete said. 'Thank you.' He backed the car up and turned round. 'Right, folks, keep your eyes peeled for a parking spot.'

* * *

As the four friends walked towards The Pines, Laura was surprised to see the number of people milling around in front of the taped-off area. There seemed to be a lot of couples and single people of a similar age to them, and quite a few policemen chatting to them. 'I wonder if there's anyone we will remember here?' she said to Anna, linking arms with her. 'It would be nice to see the girls we were with again, especially Barbara. It was a shame she didn't feel she wanted to keep in touch, but I can understand her wanting to put it all behind her and move on. We'd have been a constant reminder of the saddest time of her life.'

Anna nodded her agreement. 'Yes, we would. But I couldn't have got through all these years without you by my side, Laura. And without Mick, I don't think I would still be here. I wouldn't have wanted to live any longer.'

Laura squeezed Anna's hand. Pete's lifelong friend Mick

had been a godsend for them all during those horrendous days and long nights in that place.

Pete waved his hand at a policeman who had just finished talking to a silver-haired couple. He came across to them and introduced himself as Constable Parker. Pete told him that Anna was concerned that her lost babies' remains had been discovered here and asked who she should speak to about it. PC Parker took a pad and pen from his pocket and made a note of Anna's details along with her phone number. He pointed to another officer by the front gates to The Pines.

'If you'd like to speak with Inspector Jackson over there, he may be able to give you more information than I'm allowed to at this moment.' He paused as a cry went up and someone in the garden shouted for 'more help over here.' 'Looks like they've made a further discovery,' he said, shaking his head. 'That makes ten this morning. What the heck went on in this place all those years ago? It doesn't bear thinking about.'

Pete also shook his head as several men who were standing behind a large van hurried to join the people who were out of sight in the garden, presumably to help with the recovery process of the remains. Inspector Jackson stayed by the gates and Pete led the others across to talk to him. The inspector nodded a greeting as Pete explained why they were there and asked him if they could help in any way by telling him what they'd experienced. Laura and Anna knew where some of the small graves were located.

'It might help you to find remains quicker if our wives can tell you roughly where some of the babies were laid to rest,' Pete told the inspector. 'They were both here in 1964 for several months.'

Inspector Jackson nodded thoughtfully. 'That would be a help, if you can stick to the paths and point in the right directions,' he said. 'We don't want anyone treading on the grass and soil as the remains are so fragmented and we're in danger of missing some— Ah, just a moment,' he said as his phone rang out. He turned away and walked a few steps from the foursome, his head nodding from time to time. He ended the call and then walked back to them. 'Well, that's thrown a spanner into the works,' he said quietly, a puzzled look on his face. 'I have to go back to Macclesfield police station. The first remains that were found yesterday seem to have caused a bit of a mystery.' He took a notebook from his pocket and wrote down Pete and Laura's phone number and address, and also Mick and Anna's, even though Anna told him they had given their details to the other officer. 'Are you going back to Liverpool soon?' he asked them.

Pete nodded. 'We'll go and get a bite to eat and then set off home.'

The inspector smiled. 'That sounds like a good plan to me. I will definitely call you later and give you an update and, if necessary, we can get someone to visit the four of you and take statements in the next day or two.'

'Thank you,' Pete replied. 'We'll make sure we're under the same roof to make it easier for you.'

Anna took a deep breath and tapped the inspector on the arm, tears running down her cheeks. 'All I really want to know is if my babies have been found. I lost twin girls here, you see. I'd like to bury them properly if possible. Will you need a DNA sample from me to see if any of the remains belong to me?'

'I'm sorry to hear that. It must have been a very difficult time for you. I will definitely let you know if we need a DNA sample from you when further tests have been carried out. Believe me, we will do everything we can to help you locate your babies.' He spoke softly.

'Thank you,' Anna said, choking on a sob.

The inspector patted her arm and smiled. 'We'll be in touch soon.'

As the four walked back to the car, Pete glanced into the back of the van near the gates where the men who'd hurried to help had been standing. The door was open and revealed what looked like a pile of mud-coated tin boxes laid side by side. He shuddered and turned his head away. *Bloody nuns, couldn't even give the poor little mites proper coffins.* Mind you, wood wouldn't have lasted all this time and would have rotted away by now, he supposed. At least this way the remains would be better preserved, with a slight chance of being able to match any families that came forward. One could live in hope.

SIX

DIDSBURY, MANCHESTER

July 1964

Laura woke with a start and listened to the voices coming from the hallway, both male and female, talking in hushed tones. She glanced at her bedside clock and saw that it was just after seven o'clock. The noise of the front door opening and closing must have disturbed her; her alarm was set for eight. She was amazed that she'd even slept at all. She sat up, frowning. Was the muffled male voice Pete's? Had he come for her earlier than planned?

She got out of bed and slid her feet into slippers. Then she heard her mother's voice saying she'd make a pot of tea and telling whoever it was to go and sit in the dining room while she brewed up. Well, it definitely wouldn't be Pete then; her mother's voice was much too polite. She looked across at her small case, stood waiting by the door. She'd packed it last night after coming up to bed. She sighed. At least it was a start to her leaving home. She could get the rest of her things another time. After Pete and Angie had left, she had tried to speak to her mother, who'd locked herself in her bedroom and refused to come out. When Laura insisted they needed to talk, her reply had been curt and to the point.

'I have nothing more to say to you tonight. Go to bed and we'll talk in the morning before you go to college.'

Laura had shrugged and left it at that. She'd hurriedly packed the bag and fallen asleep still dressed in the clothes she'd worn that day, completely exhausted. Now she hurried into the bathroom, had a wash and brushed her teeth, and then took her toiletries to the bedroom to put in her case. If her mother realised she was awake and had heard her running water she'd probably assume she was getting ready to go out to college as usual. She finished her packing, fastened the catches and sat back on her heels.

The blue leather case was a bit shabby and worse for wear, but it was the one her dad used to take a change of clothes in if he was going to be away for more than a night or two and it made her feel better knowing she was taking something of him with her. She could really do with her birth certificate and was fairly certain it would be with the insurance policies in the large box her mother kept at the top of the big wardrobe in her bedroom.

She'd never had a passport, so had no need to ask for the certificate before. She couldn't honestly even remember ever seeing it. She would no doubt need it, though, to prove her age and identity if she and Pete ended up at Gretna Green to get married. Dare she go and look for it? Her mother's bedroom door had a slight squeak from a hinge that needed oiling and she would be sure to hear it opening. *Better not*, she thought. Maybe she would look later, if whoever was downstairs had come to pick up her mother to take her out. It was very early for visitors though.

She took her post office savings book from the drawer in her bedside table and put it in her handbag. There wasn't a lot of money in the account; just some of her modest Christmas and birthday monies that she'd saved for the last few years, but she and Pete would need every penny they could get their hands on, so it was better than nothing. She got dressed in light blue denim jeans and a pink short-sleeved T-shirt and slipped her feet into a pair of black casual flat shoes that would be safer to wear on the back of the scooter than heels.

Her short black leather jacket was on a hanger behind the door ready for when she left. Anything she'd been unable to fit in her case she would come back for when the house was empty. Most of her clothes were getting a bit tight round her waist now anyway and she'd need a few new baggy things for when the baby started to grow bigger. She sat down on the bed and wondered if she should go downstairs to get some breakfast and see who the early morning visitor was.

As she was trying to make up her mind, footsteps sounded on the stairs: two lots of footsteps. She frowned at a sharp knock, and then the door was thrust open and her mother appeared, closely followed by Uncle Ted, Aunty Lil's husband.

Before Laura got a chance to open her mouth, her mother looked around the room and her narrowed eyes rested on the packed suitcase. She pursed her lips and shook her head. 'Where do you think you're going with that?' she snapped, her tone as curt and unfriendly as it had been the previous night.

Laura swallowed hard and looked away from her mother's piercing gaze. 'I'm waiting for Pete to come for me,' she announced, glancing curiously at her uncle, who was looking a bit embarrassed to be standing in his niece's bedroom. 'Why is Uncle Ted here so early? Is something wrong with Aunty Lil?'

Ted shook his head but kept his mouth shut.

'Nothing is wrong with your aunt,' her mother replied. 'And you can forget about going anywhere with that boy. Ted is taking you to his house, where you will stay until a place can be found for you at a suitable establishment until you have had that, that... thing you're carrying. It will then be adopted. And then, and *only* then, will I allow you back in this house. Do you understand me, Laura?'

Laura got to her feet and stared at her mother, feeling the anger rising. 'Oh, I understand you perfectly. How dare you call my baby a thing? I can't believe you're trying to pack me off out of the way as though you're ashamed of me. My dad would be furious with you! He would have helped me, and he would never abandon me like this.'

'He'll be spinning in his grave with this state of affairs,' her mother yelled. 'And you are to have nothing more to do with that lad. I'll tell him so when he turns up, *if* he turns up. It wouldn't surprise me if you don't see him for dust now. That's what lads like him do. Use a girl and then dump her.'

'Pete would never do that to me. We love each other. We're getting married and keeping this baby whether you like it or not!' Laura yelled back. At that moment she hated her mother and needed her dad so badly.

'Ha!' her mother spat, '*Love*, don't be so ridiculous, you've no idea what love is. Get her out of my sight, Ted. I'll speak to our Lillian in a while.' She pushed Laura out of the way and left the room.

Laura burst into tears and Uncle Ted slipped an arm awkwardly round her shoulders. 'Come on, love. Let's get to my house and you can talk things over with your aunty. I think that'll be easier than saying anything more to your mother right now.' He picked up her case and led the way down the stairs and out onto the drive, and put her case in the car boot.

Laura followed him. Her mother, unsurprisingly, was nowhere to be seen. 'But Pete's coming for me at ten o'clock,' she wailed. 'I'll need to let him know where I am.'

'Don't worry about that for now. You can perhaps phone him from our place.' Uncle Ted opened the passenger door to his shiny black Jaguar and Laura climbed in and sank back into the cream leather seat. She closed her eyes and took a deep breath as he backed off the drive and headed for the posh suburb of Wilmslow.

As Laura and her uncle walked into the hallway of the smart detached house, Aunty Lil was just replacing the phone on its cradle. She turned to greet them, looking flustered. Laura spoke up first: 'I need to use your phone. I have to speak to Pete. He needs to know where I am. He'll worry if I'm not at home when he comes for me.' She burst into the tears she'd held in check on the car ride to Wilmslow. Now the floodgates were open and she was conscious of her aunt and uncle exchanging words in hushed tones.

'Uncle Ted tells me you haven't had any breakfast yet,' Aunty Lil began. 'Let's get you some tea and toast first and then we can talk.'

'No,' Laura cried. 'I want to speak to my boyfriend.'

'Come on, love. You can do that later,' Uncle Ted said, taking her arm and shaking his head at his wife as he led Laura into the lounge at the back of the house. He settled her on the sofa. Aunty Lil came into the room a few minutes later, carrying a tray with mugs and a plate of toast.

'Now come on,' she wheedled. 'It's not good for you to have an empty stomach in your, err, your condition. You need to eat. Just try, at least.'

Laura took a sip of the tea she was handed and grimaced. There was far too much sugar, but she swallowed it anyway. She shook her head. 'This is ridiculous. It's not as if I'm abandoned or even going to be an unmarried mother to shame her. Pete and I want to get married. Why is my mother being so unreasonable and hateful?'

'She thinks you're both too young for all the responsibility —' Aunty Lil began.

'But we're not,' Laura butted in. 'I'll be eighteen next

birthday and Pete will be nineteen. Loads of people get married at that age. I can go and live at Pete's house. I'm sure his mum will let me stay with them. Mum was awful to them last night. She makes me ashamed to be her daughter, never mind the other way round. And now she's bundled me off here with you and Uncle Ted to get me out of her sight. She's cruel and I hate her.'

'Now, now, let's have none of that kind of talk,' Aunty Lil said. 'She's only doing what she thinks is best. I've spoken to my neighbour across the avenue who works for Cheshire Social Services in Macclesfield and she thinks we can get you a place at The Pines in Bollington. It's a nice mother-and-baby home, I believe. They'll look after you until you're ready to go back home. They're going to ring me in an hour or so to let me know there's definitely a place for you and then Uncle Ted will take you over there.'

Laura stared at her aunt in horror. 'No, you can't do this,' she yelled. 'Pete will go mad. You can't hide me away.' She burst into tears and made to run out of the room, but Uncle Ted caught her by the arm and led her back to the sofa.

'It's all arranged, love,' he said, sitting down beside her. 'It's for the best, you'll see that one day.'

SEVEN

BOLLINGTON, CHESHIRE

July 1964

Exhausted from crying, Laura sank numbly down on the narrow bed in the large bedroom and looked around. It was only late morning, but she felt like it had been the longest day of her life. There were four beds in total and, judging by the personal items on two of the bedside tables opposite, those beds were already occupied. Beside each bed was a narrow wardrobe with three drawers underneath.

The room was fresh and clean, with plain white walls and paintwork. Pale green cotton curtains matching the bedspreads hung at the bay window. Home-made rag rugs in stripes of pink and green lay by each bed on the polished wooden floor.

It looked pleasant enough, but was deathly quiet. There appeared to be no sign of life. A plump, middle-aged woman, her red hair fastened up into a clumsy French pleat with straggly curls breaking free around her face and serious green eyes that didn't quite meet Laura's, had brought her up to the bedroom and then had vanished as soon as she'd shown Laura

which bed was hers. She'd told Laura that she was Miss
Greaves, the assistant housekeeper, before she'd hurried on her
way, closing the door quietly behind her.

The nun, Sister Celia, who had booked her in and taken her
details after abruptly dismissing Uncle Ted, had only spoken to
her for about five minutes and then sent her off with Miss
Greaves. Aunty Lil hadn't let her call Pete before they left as
she had told her that she didn't want to go against Laura's mother's instructions, and now it was eleven thirty and he would
have been to her house and her mother would no doubt have
packed him off, if indeed she had even opened the door to him.
Laura couldn't even write to him as she had no pens, paper or
stamps with her.

Hopefully, someone sharing the room might be able to help
her. But where was everyone? The other girls must be else-
where in the large house, maybe working or something. Hopefully, someone would come for her soon and tell her what
happened next. She walked across to the bay window and
looked down at the large gardens to the front of the property.
There was no one in sight there either. Hopefully, someone
would come and get her soon, maybe at lunchtime.

As she stared into the distance she spotted a large dark-blue
car making its way slowly along winding Dumbah Lane,
turning onto The Pines' drive and stopping by the main doors
below. A man and woman got out of the front seats and the
woman opened the back passenger door and pulled out a young
girl, who staggered slightly as she righted herself by holding on
to the car door. The girl looked pale and frightened and she was
crying.

The woman was wagging a warning finger in her face as the
man took a small case out of the car boot. The woman got back
into the car without speaking to the girl again as the man practi-
cally frogmarched her to the door and handed over the case to

someone Laura couldn't see; most probably the same nun who had booked her in, she thought. She went back to sit on her bed and before long, heard someone coming up the stairs and the door opening. Nodding to her, Miss Greaves ushered in the girl Laura had seen from the window before pointing to the bed next to Laura's. She smiled at both girls and then left the room.

Laura smiled at the girl, who smiled shyly back. 'Hello, I'm Laura,' she said. 'I've just arrived here too.'

The girl, whose rich auburn hair hung down her back in a single fat plait, nodded. 'Anna,' she introduced herself and turned her blue tear-filled eyes to Laura. 'It looks like we're in the same boat. I feel totally abandoned.'

'Me too.' Laura nodded her agreement. 'I'm still in shock, and wondering what the heck I'm doing here.' She paused as a light knocking sounded at the door and went to open it. Miss Greaves entered, carrying a tray with mugs of tea and plates of sandwiches.

'Sorry I couldn't open the door myself,' she apologised. 'Had to use me elbow to knock to let you know I was there. Sister Celia said to bring you up a bit of lunch. She also said you're to both have a rest this afternoon and then you can meet some of the other girls at supper tonight.'

'Thank you,' Laura and Anna chorused as Miss Greaves quickly left the room after depositing the tray on Laura's bedside table.

Anna stared after the woman and then shook her head. 'She's a bit of an odd one, don't you think? She looks anywhere but at your face when she's talking to you.'

Laura nodded. 'Yes, she is a bit odd. She didn't look me in the eye at all when she brought me up here. Maybe she's under instructions from whoever is in charge not to get too close or friendly with any of us for some reason.'

Anna shrugged. 'Yes, possibly. I've no idea what to expect of this place or the nuns and staff. I really don't want to be here. I shouldn't be here at all.' Tears tumbled down her cheeks and Laura instinctively reached out to hug her.

'Nor I,' she said. 'But come on, let's have this tea and sandwiches she's brought us and then we can have a bit of a chat. I think once we've got our heads around things by talking, we may feel better and a bit more able to cope as well.'

Laura lay on her bed propped up by the two thin pillows she'd been provided with. The time was now almost four in the afternoon and she was struggling to stay awake. She looked across at Anna, who was curled up fast asleep, her pale face tear-stained. The poor girl was worn out from what she'd been forced to endure over the last few weeks. Anna, who was only sixteen years old and from the Liverpool suburb of Woolton, had poured her heart out and told Laura that her middle-class parents were ashamed of her and had brought her here.

They refused to allow her to stay at home any longer. They'd told her they were embarrassed by her condition. Anna's boyfriend Tony had been killed two months ago while out riding his motorbike. Shortly after his funeral a distraught Anna had realised she was pregnant with his baby. As soon as her mother had guessed the situation, and before Anna had the opportunity to tell Tony's family, her parents had held her a prisoner in her own home until they found a place for her at The Pines.

She'd pleaded with them to at least find her somewhere local to have her baby, but they refused. They told her they would tell their neighbours, and any family members who asked after her, that she was doing a cadet nursing course in Manchester, with residential accommodation provided by the hospital. She had been forbidden to contact any member of Tony's family and the staff here had also been told that she was not to send any letters to anyone.

Laura wondered now how the devil she was going to let Pete know that she was here if the staff were going to be monitoring every move. She also wondered if they'd been instructed to monitor *her* letter-writing activities too. On the drive over here, she couldn't actually recall seeing any nearby shops to buy stationery and stamps from, or any postboxes, or telephone boxes for that matter, in the near vicinity either. She was certain that Pete would be frantic by now. She had to let him know where she was; somehow she would need to find a way in the next day or two.

Her thoughtful reverie was broken by the bedroom door opening quietly and a tall, dark-haired girl stuck her head round it. The girl smiled and Laura smiled back.

'Hello,' the girl began, and then saw Anna was asleep. She lowered her voice as she continued, 'Sorry to disturb you but I need to grab something from my bedside drawers.' She hurried across the room, rooted in the top drawer and popped something into her dress pocket. 'Rennies,' she said. 'I've got shocking heartburn and they don't like us taking anything, they'd rather we suffered, but my friend told me to get some before I came here, so I brought some with me.'

Laura smiled. 'Very wise, and you're not disturbing me,' she said and nodded towards Anna, 'and Anna's out for the count.'

'Probably the stress and trauma of coming here,' the girl said. 'We're all the same at first. Crying enough tears to fill a lake. I'm Barbara, by the way.'

'Nice to meet you, Barbara. I'm Laura and that of course is Anna. We're the latest and only recruits today, I believe.'

Barbara nodded. 'You are. We were told this morning that we had two new girls joining us. It's nice to meet you too, but I'm sorry it has to be in here and not somewhere a bit more sociable. Still, we'll get one another through this. Let's face it, we're all the support any of us have got. I've been here six weeks now and Lydia in the bed next to mine has been here for five months. Her baby is due next week, so I'm glad I've got new room-mates to take her place when she leaves.'

'Are there many girls in residence at the moment?' Laura asked. 'It seems awfully quiet. The only people we've seen so far are Sister Celia, who welcomed us in, and Miss Greaves.'

'There are two more rooms like this, with four girls in each right now,' Barbara said. 'Sister Celia is the friendliest of the five nuns that reside and work here. I think they make her do all the booking in so that it lulls us into a false sense of feeling that this is an okay place to be. But don't let that fool you. It's a horrible place, really. Being here is like serving a prison sentence, except we've done nothing wrong and we're not locked in cells all day. Although we might as well be, for all the bloomin' freedom we get.'

'Crikey,' said Laura, 'I didn't realise it was going to be this bad.'

'I know. I thought you'd better be prepared. Anyway, I'd better go back down to the kitchen or they'll wonder where I am. We'll chat more when we come up to bed later and you can tell us how you two nice girls ended up in The Pines. Oh, and by the way – Miss Greaves, or Olive as we call her when there's no nuns about, she's a nice enough soul, but she's not all there, you know.' She tapped the top of her head.

'Got a bit of brain damage at birth, apparently. She's not as old as she looks either and she came in here about five years ago to have a baby that sadly didn't survive. She had no home or family to go back to, so they kept her on to help with the house-keeping and she's been here ever since. She's very quiet and keeps herself to herself, but she's a great cook and she makes a damn good cake.'

'Well, her lunchtime sandwiches were very nice,' Laura said. 'She just seemed to be really shy.'

Barbara nodded. 'She is. Listen out for the bell ringing at six o'clock,' she added as she made for the door. 'That's the supper bell. Olive may come up to show you where to go but, if not, come downstairs and make your way to the dining room. Just follow the girls you'll see on their way there. I'm helping Cook and Olive to make tonight's meal, but I'll see you in there later.'

'Thanks, Barbara, and goodbye for now,' Laura called after her.

EIGHT

WEST DERBY, LIVERPOOL

May 2015

Pete hung up the phone and made his way back into the lounge, where Laura, Anna and Mick were seated. 'That was Inspector Jackson with a bit of an update for us,' he announced.

Anna jumped to her feet, her hand on her chest. 'Did they say if they've been able to identify the remains?' she asked.

Pete shook his head. 'He didn't say that, no. But what he did say is that he's coming to see us tomorrow morning at ten thirty. Can you two be back here for that time?'

Mick nodded. 'We can. Let's hope the news he's got is good. Not that deceased babies is ever *good* news, of course. But at least it may give some families a bit of closure to bury their own flesh and blood.'

'If they've definitely got my girls' remains, I will give them a proper resting place and a nice service,' Anna said. 'I'm going to ask Tony's mum if they can go in the grave with him. I think it's only right and proper that we do that for them. I'm sure she will agree with me.'

Laura gave Anna a hug. 'I think that's a wonderful idea.

And it will be so lovely for you that you can take them some nice flowers on their birthday too.'

Mick smiled. 'Come on, let's get you home,' he said to Anna. 'We'll see these two in the morning. Hope you both manage to get some sleep.'

Pete saw them out and shook his head as he came back into the lounge. 'Poor Anna, what an awful ordeal for her to go through. And for you too, love. I know how very close you are. But at least we know that somewhere out there, our son is hopefully alive and well. If only we could find him. There must be a way these days, surely. I know we've done all we think we can in our search, but with modern technology and all that, it's got to be easier than it was years ago when we first started looking.'

Laura sighed. 'Maybe we should try again. I'd hate him to think we didn't ever try and find him. He may have no idea he was adopted. We never got the chance to name him or register him. I hardly even got to see him, just that glimpse as the bloody nuns rushed him away.'

Pete nodded. 'Evil bastards, and I don't care what anyone thinks of me for calling them names. They robbed us of our son and I can never forgive them for that. He must be abroad; got to be the USA or Canada, or maybe even Australia as we've exhausted all avenues here. But with no name or birth certificate or any documentation whatsoever to go on, I don't know where we'd start. We were told when we started looking that everything from The Pines was purposefully destroyed when the authorities closed it, so God knows how we'll do it. Anyway, you go on up to bed, love. I'll bring you a nice cuppa up in a few minutes.' He kissed Laura and hugged her. 'We'll find him one day, I promise you.'

* * *

As Laura left the room, Pete put the kettle on and made a pot of tea using tea bags. Laura hated tea leaves in the bottom of her cup and always had done, as long as he'd known her. His mind went back to that long-ago morning when he'd gone to her house on his scooter at ten, as he'd promised, to collect her to go away with him, so they could get married. Her hateful mother had answered the door and told him that Laura wasn't at home.

When he'd demanded to know her whereabouts she'd told him that it was not his business to know where Laura was and that her daughter didn't want anything more to do with him, which he knew for sure was a blatant lie. He'd yelled at her that he had every right to know as Laura was expecting his baby and they loved one another. She'd cringed at that and he was conscious of next door's net curtains twitching as he'd demanded once more to know where Laura was.

She'd slammed the door in his face and that was the last time he'd set eyes on her. He'd ridden his scooter home, tears blinding him. He had no idea where to look for Laura and his own mum hadn't been much help as she'd said she still felt insulted from the previous night's fiasco with Laura's mother. She'd told him to put it all behind him and he'd soon find another girl. That getting married was not the right thing to do, he was far too young, and she and his dad were withdrawing their permission anyway. He'd felt so lost and alone, until— Pete tried to interrupt his own thoughts, not wanting to go back over that dark time.

Inspector Jackson and a young policewoman, who introduced herself as PC Miles, arrived just before ten thirty and Laura invited them to sit in the lounge. Anna and Mick had already arrived and were eagerly waiting to hear the latest news.

'Can I get anyone a tea or coffee?' Pete asked. 'Kettle's just boiled.'

'Thank you, that would be very nice,' Inspector Jackson replied. 'We've been on duty since first thing this morning and then with the drive over to Liverpool, we missed our break. Two coffees, one with sugar and one without, please.'

'Same here for us,' Anna said. 'Thanks, Pete.'

Laura followed her husband into the kitchen, sliced a Swiss roll and opened a packet of chocolate digestives. She arranged the cake and biscuits on a large plate while Pete saw to the coffee-brewing.

Back in the lounge, Laura told everyone to help themselves and sat in an armchair, while Pete sat on the floor beside her. She could feel her heart hammering in her chest and wondered what this latest news could be.

Inspector Jackson had carried a box file into the house and he balanced it on his knees while he took a few sips of coffee. Then he put down his mug and opened the file. He took a sheet of paper out and looked at it with eyebrows raised before he spoke.

'There are a few reasons we wanted to speak to you all today as we have something very strange going on with the discoveries at The Pines. If you can help us by throwing a bit of light on things, it will assist our investigations. But I must ask that you keep anything we discuss here to yourselves for the time being. I actually feel this is going to go a lot deeper than we originally thought. We are now beginning to think that criminal activities involving newborn babies may have continued for several decades.'

Anna gasped. 'What, you think the babies were murdered rather than stillborn?'

He shook his head. 'No, it's not that. But I have to tell you, as this information may be going out on the ITV regional evening news programme tonight, I would rather you hear it from us first. We have had a forensics team working all night long on the boxes that we found and removed from the site yesterday and so far there are no traces of human remains amongst them.'

A collective gasp sounded from Laura, Pete, Anna and Mick.

'What?' Pete said. 'So what the hell are they then?'

Inspector Jackson continued. 'It would appear they are the remains of small animals. Possibly squirrels, kittens, and even a couple of rat skeletons have been identified. There are ten more boxes to check through this morning, which makes a total of fifty up to now, before an announcement can be made, but what we have so far discovered makes us think that the small animals were buried as a substitute for the children that were supposed to have died.'

'Well, I'll be blowed,' Mick said softly.

The inspector continued, 'After all, at birth it's our theory the baby would have been whisked away, declared deceased without the mother actually seeing it and a hasty funeral arranged. I'm making an educated guess here, so please correct me if I'm wrong, but it's my opinion that the young mothers would have been so traumatised by events that they would have been most likely not fit enough to attend the so-called burial. Therefore they'd have had no knowledge that their children were quite possibly still alive when they were sent home from The Pines.'

Laura jumped to her feet and grabbed Anna by the hand. Her friend's face was as white as the handkerchief Mick had been using to wipe away her tears as they tumbled down her cheeks.

'You know what this could mean, don't you?' Laura gasped.

Anna nodded, wide-eyed with shock. 'My babies,' she cried, 'my babies may have been born alive. They may *still* be alive and grown up now. Those evil witches stole them and gave them away. They must have sold them,' she yelled in the direction of Inspector Jackson, startling him.

Anna continued, 'Just like they sold all the babies who were alive and who were supposed to have been legally adopted. We were sure they sold them, but we weren't allowed to question it. I never saw a sign of any paperwork to say my babies had died, I just had the nuns' word for it and that they'd held a little funeral service for them right away before they packed me off to that bloody loony asylum! There was nothing wrong with me other than I was grieving and they kept me doped up. They were evil.'

'And I never saw any proof that our son was adopted officially,' Laura said. 'I was told he'd gone to an adoptive family and that I'd signed the papers giving my consent – which I know I didn't do, I promised Pete I wouldn't. They'd knocked me out with a mask over my face that contained some drug or other and I never even got to hold him or anything. I caught a glimpse of dark hair, heard a cry and he'd gone. I don't remember anything else. I've dreamt of him so many times, our son, our little baby boy.'

Laura put her head on Pete's shoulder and both wept for the child they'd lost.

NINE

BOLLINGTON, CHESHIRE

July 1964

After supper and an introduction to the other girls, Laura and Anna sat side by side in a small chapel area attached to the back of the house. Sister Celia read a short sermon, which was followed by a service of prayers and hymn-singing. The words of the sermon shocked Laura as it was about lack of morals and how the girls in the congregation had all committed a sin that God would find it hard to forgive for the rest of their lives.

They would need to repent by working hard during their time at The Pines to atone for those sins. Laura had been brought up a Protestant and had attended Sunday School at the local church regularly as a youngster, but had never been preached to like this before. She wasn't aware that she had committed any sins; all she'd done was fall in love with Pete. How could loving someone be a sin? If that was the case, half the world was regularly committing sins, for goodness' sake. And she and Pete wanted to get married; it was her horrible mum who wouldn't let them.

She glanced across to where the five nuns were seated.

They all looked hard-faced and miserable; even Sister Celia looked glum now she was down from the pulpit and back in her seat. They looked like they were sucking lemons or had a bad smell under their nose, as her dad used to say about her mum at times. He called her mum a God-botherer when she went to church on Sunday mornings and tried to persuade him that he should go with her.

He always refused, saying the odd Sunday morning he wasn't working was meant for reading his *News of the World*, a newspaper she did not approve of, and enjoying bacon butties with a big mug of tea. He told her mother that, if going to church so many times was the cause of her miserable face and bad moods, he wanted nothing to do with religion. He would go mad if he could see his daughter now, Laura thought. She breathed a sigh of relief when the girls were dismissed and told to go quietly to their rooms, where they were to remain for the rest of the night, with the lights out at ten.

'Thank God for that,' Anna muttered as they followed Barbara and Lydia to their shared room. 'I'm not a Catholic. What was all that about, and do we have to listen to it every night?'

Barbara shook her head. 'It's only when they admit new recruits and at weekends. That was for the benefit of you two tonight, for your sins, don't you know?' she teased with a smile. 'We're not Catholics either, but this place is part-financed by the Catholic Church and the rest comes from the pockets of our parents or guardians.'

'Oh dear, now that *will* please my mother,' Laura chipped in as they entered the bedroom, and then added, 'Or rather, it serves her right. All she had to do last night was give me her permission to marry my Pete and I'd be out of her hair by now and then she wouldn't be out of pocket.' Her eyes filled as she thought of Pete and how upset and angry he would be by now. He would be desperate to know where she was.

Barbara reached into the cupboard of her bedside table and pulled out a small transistor radio: 'Let's have a bit of music on.' She tuned in to Radio Luxembourg. The reception was crackly and faded in and out but it was better than nothing. Helen Shapiro's deep tones filled the room as the four girls joined in with 'Walking Back to Happiness'.

The song came to an end and Lydia got herself as comfortable as she could on the narrow bed with her pillows wedged behind her aching back. She unpinned her long dark hair that had been fastened up all day and sighed. 'Oh, that's better,' she said. 'I can't wait for this baby to arrive. I'm exhausted after being on my feet all day, cleaning their ladyships' rooms. That Sister Ursula is the most untidy person on the planet. So much for the saying Cleanliness is Next to Godliness. What a load of old codswallop! She's downright filthy and her room stinks of sweaty old shoes.'

Laura shook her head and frowned. 'Why did you have to clean the nuns' rooms? Don't they have cleaning staff here to do that?'

'We *are* the cleaning staff, I'm afraid, Laura,' Barbara told her. 'The nuns do sod all apart from sit around while we wait on them hand and foot, preach at us, and deliver the babies as they arrive.'

'The nuns deliver the babies?' Anna said, looking shocked. 'Don't we get midwives and doctors?'

'Only if there's an emergency will they call a doctor,' Barbara replied. 'Two of the nuns are supposedly midwives, but I don't reckon they are properly qualified.'

'Oh God, I don't like the sound of that,' Laura said. 'Even more reason to get out of here. I need to let Pete know where I am, he'll be going crazy. I need to phone him or send him a letter as soon as possible.'

'That's not going to be easy,' Lydia said. 'They watch us like hawks. Next time I see any stationery lying around in the offices, I'll try and nab you some paper and envelopes. But I'm not sure how we'll get a stamp. Olive may be able to help us there though; she sometimes takes the post to the post office for the nuns and also collects and distributes the occasional letters to the girls here.'

'Thank you,' Laura said. 'Pete was coming for me this morning on his scooter, and we were going to go to Gretna Green and get married, but my mother sent me off to my aunt and uncle's first thing and then I was brought here and I haven't been able to let him know what's happened.'

'Lucky you to have a boyfriend who cares enough to want to marry you,' Barbara said. 'I wish that was my story. My ex has got himself engaged to another girl after making me all sorts of promises if I'd go all the way with him. He's told her that this baby isn't his and that I'm lying, and the silly cow believes him. My mother packed me off here as she said she's disgusted with me and I can't go home unless I get it adopted.'

'I'm so sorry,' Laura said as Barbara's eyes filled with tears. 'That's awful of him to treat you like that.'

'Oh, that's only half the tale, it gets better,' Barbara said. 'Phil joined the RAF just as I found out I was pregnant. We'd been together about eight months at the time. Then he sent me a letter saying he'd met another girl before he left home and he wanted to break it off with me. I wrote back and pleaded with him not to finish with me as I was expecting his baby.'

'That was brave of you,' said Anna quietly.

'Well, it didn't do any good as he didn't reply to that letter and in desperation, I wrote to *Two Way Family Favourites*, the BBC forces radio programme, to ask them to play a request from me to him. And they actually bloomin' well played it a couple of Sundays later. They read out both our names and said that he should listen to the words of the song. An hour later, there was a hammering at the front door and my mum went to answer. It was her, the new girlfriend, and she said she'd heard my ridiculous radio request and that Phil didn't want to know me and that I should just get lost. And then in front of my mum, who had no idea about my pregnancy, she pokes me in the stomach and said I should stop blaming him for that as well. It wasn't his baby, it was my own mess to sort out. Then she flounced off; my mum went bananas, and here I am.'

'Blimey, what a tale,' Laura said. 'I'm so sorry. I don't know what else to say.'

Anna propped herself up on her bed and looked across with a frown. 'Can I just ask what song you requested, seeing as it made the new girlfriend mad enough to come to your house?'

Barbara sighed and then gave a sheepish half-smile. 'Well, it was daft of me really, it was Neil Sedaka's "Let's Go Steady Again" but it didn't bloody well work, did it? Thanks a lot, Neil!' She started to giggle and the others joined in.

Lydia groaned and hugged her moving bump. 'Now we've woken it up, it'll be kicking my bladder all flippin' night. I know Barbara's story isn't really a laughing matter, but we needed that bit of a giggle, girls. It's done us good. I'm glad you two are here because I'll be gone very soon and she needs good company to keep her spirits up for the next few months.'

'Where will you go?' Laura asked. 'I mean, after you've given birth.'

Lydia shrugged. 'I have absolutely no idea at the moment. My plan is back to Buxton, I hope. I was a third-year student nurse at the Devonshire Royal Hospital there and I'm hoping I can go back and finish my training.' She patted her bump. 'This is my own fault; the result of a stupid one-night stand after a party. I can't keep it, as I have nowhere to live. My home is the nurses' home at the hospital. I'm not close to my family and they don't even know I'm here. I'll just have to put it all behind me and hope for the best. There'll be no handsome knight on a shiny scooter coming to rescue me, I'm afraid, but hopefully there'll be a nice family to adopt this little one.'

They all nodded. Laura brushed away a tear and sighed.

Anna shook her head. 'Sadly, there will be no handsome knight for me either.' She told Lydia and Barbara the tale she'd told Laura earlier. 'But, like Laura,' she added, 'I'm hoping there will be a way to get word to Tony's family, who might come to my rescue one day and help me to keep and bring up my baby.'

TEN

BOLLINGTON, CHESHIRE

August 1964

As the first two weeks dragged slowly by, Laura grew angrier and more frustrated at the situation she was in. There never seemed to be a minute where the girls were not being watched over by one nun or another. The only time they could relax and talk for a while was at night before lights out at ten. Each small group of girls had permission to take a fifteen-minute morning walk for exercise around the large gardens, sticking to the paths only. A nun followed them at a distance almost all the way round, so Laura couldn't even check to see if there was a gap in a hedge that she might be able to squeeze through to get away from the place.

There'd been no phone calls or letters from her family, not that she'd been expecting any contact from her mother, but it would have been nice to know that her aunt and uncle at least were thinking about her from time to time. Maybe they would, eventually – it was still early days; but already she felt as if she'd been here forever. Her college friends would wonder where she was, especially Mary, who she caught the bus with each day and in whom she'd confided her pregnancy fears – unless Pete had spoken to her at the youth club and let her know she was no longer at home. But Mary would have no clue as to where Laura was to write to her. Anna, pulling on the sleeve of her cotton top, brought her out of her reverie and she turned to see what her friend wanted.

They were in the big laundry room today, washing bedding from various girls' rooms, and it was hot and steamy. It was backbreaking work, pushing the wet sheets through the heavy mangles before hanging them outside on washing lines to dry.

'What did you say?' Laura asked above the noise of the washing machines, where more sheets were swishing around and around.

'You were miles away just then,' Anna said. 'You look a bit pale. Are you okay?'

Laura sighed and ran her fingers through the damp hair that flopped into her eyes. 'I'm fine, just sick and tired of this dump. Is it nearly break time? I could murder a cuppa.'

Anna glanced up at the clock on the wall. 'Ten more minutes. Thank God— Uh-oh, naughty, naughty, we mustn't blaspheme.' She smirked and looked over her shoulder towards where Sister Benedict was telling another girl off for taking a few minutes to sit down on an old wooden stool. The poor girl looked fit to drop and was very heavily pregnant. She was also crying.

'What a witch,' Laura whispered. 'Poor Carol, she's worn out.'

Anna nodded. 'They treat us like slaves. I can't stand much more of this.'

'You and me both,' Laura said. 'Right, let's get these sheets on the line and it'll be time to have our break.'

. . .

Barbara and Lydia were already seated at a table near the back of the dining room and they waved to Anna and Laura to come and join them.

'You go and sit down,' Laura said to Anna, 'and I'll get our brews and snacks.' She smiled at Olive Greaves, who was pouring out the tea into mugs from a large stainless-steel teapot. Laura's heart sank as she saw there were no tea strainers lying on the countertops, which meant tea leaves in the bottom of the mug. But beggars couldn't be choosers: she'd just have to be careful with the last few mouthfuls.

'Would you like to try a bit of my banana bread?' Olive said. 'It's the first time I've made it, so I can't promise it will be good, but it smells nice enough.' All this was said without her even looking up at Laura.

Laura smiled. 'Of course, Miss Greaves, thank you. I'm sure it will taste lovely. Can I take a slice for Anna as well, please?'

A slight smile crossed Olive's face as she nodded and placed two small slices of the cake onto a plate.

'Thank you,' Laura said, hooking her finger through two mug handles and picking up the plate.

'Here, let me help you, you'll drop that tea and scald yourself if you're not careful. You need to use both hands.' Olive shot out from behind the countertop, took the plate from Laura and carried it across to the table where Anna was sitting. Sister Ursula, standing by the window on dining room duty, scowled in her direction as she scurried back to her place behind the teapot, head bowed down again, before Laura could thank her.

'Blimey, that's the first time I've ever seen Olive helping anyone in here. She's usually so scared of her own shadow,' Lydia said as Laura sat down beside her. 'She'll no doubt get a right rollicking from Stinky Nun later, the poor woman.'

'Bless her, she actually smiled when she gave me the cake,' Laura said. 'She seems to be not just shy, but very lonely as well.

Wish we could help her, but I think she's just too much in awe of the nuns to speak to us outside of the dining room.'

Lydia sighed and nodded her agreement. She nudged Laura and pointed to the deep pocket of the baggy tunic top that covered her large and now overdue baby bump. Laura glanced down and her eyes opened wide as she saw stationery tucked in there. 'I have a plan,' Lydia mouthed. 'Tell you at bedtime.'

Laura smiled and took a sip of tea, a thrill of excitement running through her. It had been several days since Lydia said she'd try to get her some paper and envelopes if there was ever a chance. This could be it; the start of her road to freedom. Even the thoughts of an afternoon of stinking laundry duties couldn't quell the feelings of hope bubbling inside her right now.

As Laura and Anna dashed back to their room after the evening meal, they spotted Barbara and Lydia halfway up the wide stair-case leading up from the hallway. Barbara was helping Lydia, who seemed to be in pain. Laura rushed on ahead and opened their bedroom door. Barbara helped Lydia on to her bed and propped her up with pillows borrowed from all four beds, and Anna closed the door, after first making sure no nuns had followed and was lurking in the corridor.

'Right,' Barbara said, switching on her little transistor radio to try and prevent any sound they made from reaching the corri-dor. 'Lydia's in labour, but she was determined to tell you her plan before they cart her off to the delivery room on the top floor. We may not see her again for a few days and, even then, they may send her away before we get the chance to catch up so this could be it.'

Lydia nodded and took a deep breath. 'I've only just started with the pains but I think it's on its way. It's a week overdue so I guess this will be it. The nuns don't know yet, so bear with me.' She rooted in her pocket and pushed the stationery she'd been hiding under a large hanky towards Laura and Anna. 'Sorry, it's a bit creased now, and I couldn't get much, but there's enough for you to write your escape letters on and if you address the envelopes, I will hide them in my case and post them as soon as I get back to Buxton. There's some torn lining at the bottom in there that they can be hidden inside, just in case the nuns open it to have a nosy.'

'Lydia, you're a star, thank you,' Anna said.

Lydia smiled briefly and took a deep breath as another wave of pain hit her. She sighed and continued. 'Not sure they'll open my case, but we'll take no chances and I doubt they'll unpack everything when they're on the verge of getting shot of me. Now I know you want to write to Pete, Laura, but his mother might pick up the letter before he sees it and chuck it away. So, rather than waste this opportunity, have you got a trusted friend you can write to and put a letter for Pete in the envelope too? Someone you know who will give the letter to him?'

'Yes, I think I do, thank you,' said Laura, thinking fast.

'I don't have a clue how he would write back to you, or even if the nuns open the letters sent here before they are handed out to the girls. I suppose they do if they suspect any are from someone a girl shouldn't be in touch with. Olive has the job of distributing any mail we get, which is good. We'll have to take a chance now and hope that they don't open any replies. I'll give you my address in Buxton – Pete could write to you and send it to me and then I could write to you here and send any letters from him tucked in with mine. I know it sounds a bit long-winded and complicated and it's a lot to take in, but I've been thinking about it for days and wondering how the heck I can help you both.' Lydia paused and took a deep breath, a look of pain crossing her face.

'Anna has Tony's family to turn to,' she carried on after the pain passed, 'and you have Pete, who wants to stand by you. It's wrong that you're both incarcerated in this hellhole like no one cares when we know they do—' She stopped again and groaned. 'Agh, bloody hell that was a strong one! Right, you lot get on with the escape plan while I'm still around. Barbara has my case keys to get the letters out of sight. I might not get a chance to see you again before I go, they don't like us to have further contact, probably so we can't tell tales, so good luck.'

ELEVEN

WEST DERBY, LIVERPOOL

June 2015

Laura and Pete's daughters, Rosie and Penny, sat side by side on the sofa as their dad explained what had happened with the discovery of the remains at The Pines. Laura had called her girls earlier and asked them to come over as she and their dad wanted to talk to them about something. Neither had seen the news, and, as they got their updates on social media these days, rather than watch TV or read a newspaper, they were oblivious to the recent goings-on in Bollington. As soon as they were old enough to understand, the girls had been told that they had an older brother who had been adopted against their parents' will and they also knew that their parents had tried to find him, without success.

'So what does this all mean, exactly?' Rosie asked. 'Do you think Anna's babies may have been born alive then?'

Laura shrugged. 'There's a possibility. There have been no remains found that belong to her, or anyone else for that matter. It's taking a lot of getting our heads around things at the moment, which is why Dad and I wanted to speak with you privately, in case you think we're ignoring you when we don't always answer the phone or we're out a lot at the moment. I just wish we knew how the heck we can go about finding out where our lost children are. If only the nuns had handed over our files when The Pines was being sold and cleared out.'

'How do you know they didn't?' Penny asked. 'They should really have been handed to social services, although the police will no doubt have checked that out. But could they have been given to the nearest Catholic church maybe, and a priest or whoever is in charge has still got them?'

'Well, like you say, the police will be looking into all that, I should think,' Pete said. 'But it wouldn't surprise me if it's all been destroyed so that no one can be blamed for whatever went on in that place.'

'But someone with a conscience might come forward now the news is out there,' Penny said. 'A staff member maybe.'

Laura shook her head. 'There were no staff employed, just us girls and the nuns, who we were slaves to. Oh, and a lovely lady a few years older than us girls called Olive, who did a lot of the cooking. She was very nice, but really shy and reserved – and I wouldn't be surprised if she's passed away by now, she wasn't that well.' Laura took a deep breath and tried to focus on more positive things. 'Anyway, we found each other again in the end, and maybe one day we'll find your brother Paul too,' she said, tears shining in her eyes as she smiled at Pete, who gave her a hug and dropped a kiss on her lips.

'Get a room, you two,' Rosie said with a laugh. 'I just can't believe what those nuns did to you. It beggars belief that such a home could exist, it really does.'

Laura sighed. 'It was a very different way of life back then and there were many homes like that. And most of us were so young. Our parents were a different kettle of fish to how we've been with you two. Although your dad's parents soon came round, as you know.'

'You're not kidding.' Penny rolled her eyes. 'I shouldn't say this, as she was my grandmother, but your mum sounded awful, Mum; such a control freak and nasty with it compared to Dad's mum. But your dad sounded a lovely man and I do wish we'd got to know him.'

'I wish you'd known him too,' Laura said with a sigh. 'My dad was the loveliest man. He died so young. I always talk to his photograph and tell him all about you. Well, wherever he is, I'm sure he's watching over us and maybe one day he'll guide us to finding our Paul.'

'Have you thought of trying to find him via social media, Mum?' Penny asked. 'There are groups where you can look for lost relatives or adopted children on Facebook.'

'Really?' Laura chewed her lip. She had a Facebook account but only really used it to wish people happy birthday or commiserate if someone had passed away. 'How does that work then?'

Penny took her phone from her handbag and logged on to her Facebook account. She found the group she was looking for and showed it to Laura and Pete. 'See, all these people are trying to find their mothers, or the mothers are trying to find their long-lost children. This mother-and-baby home we're looking at now was on the Isle of Man. They seem to have had some success stories. There are quite a few pictures of reunions. Maybe you and Anna could start a group for The Pines.'

Laura looked at Pete, who was scrolling down Penny's phone with interest. 'What do you think, Pete?'

'Hmm,' he said. 'Well, social media wasn't around when we began our search for Paul. I suppose we should have a think about it. The only trouble is, we're back to square one in that we have no surnames or anything to go on. We never got the chance to give him a name or register his birth and get a birth certificate. We called him Paul because your mum was a Paul McCartney fan in her youth. Your mum's cousin Fliss is the solicitor who helped us initially and she said we had reached a dead end with no paper trail. There was simply nowhere else to turn. All we've had since is the hope that one day out of the blue he'd come knocking at our door, but I guess that's never going to happen, as he'll have no clue who his birth parents are.'

Penny nodded. 'Yep, I know. But you know his date of birth, you two are white British and you know where he was born. It's a start, Dad, a small one, but it's still a start. If by any chance he's out there looking for you, if he's been told he's adopted and from which part of the UK, a group like this would give him something to go on. And there's the Ancestry company for people doing family trees as well. They do DNA testing and that can link you with possible family members from all over the place. You just never know if he's been trying to do the same thing, if he's been searching for you.'

Pete took a deep breath. 'It's a nice thought. Let your mum and me have a good think about it. It's a lot to take in at the moment, but it might just work out. The police will be in touch again very soon and we will need to make sure we don't cause an issue, if they have a legal case going on with anything they may have linked to The Pines. If they say we should go ahead, then maybe you could come over one day and help your mum and Anna to set up a group.'

'Wouldn't it be wonderful if Anna could find her daughters?' Laura said, her eyes filling. 'She was never able to have any more children after she was so badly damaged from the twins' birth. Those nuns have a lot to answer for. They even denied her a doctor and she should have had a Caesarean in hospital, but they wouldn't hear of it and nearly killed her in the process. And Tony's old mum would be over the moon if they were found. She's getting on now and all this would make her last few years an absolute joy. I think a group like the one you've showed us would be great.'

'Mum, maybe you could reunite with some of the girls you made friends with while you were in there as well?' said Penny.

'Yes, that's a good thought. We never got to say goodbye to or keep in touch with them as they wouldn't allow us any contact with each other once a baby was born. They isolated the new mums and then shipped them out very quickly. When I think back now, I'm sure it was to keep us quiet so we couldn't tell tales to the ones who were still waiting to give birth. I almost lost contact with Anna once they transferred her to the psychiatric home, but thankfully, Olive knew where they'd sent her as it was the same one she was in for a while.'

Laura shook her head sadly. It was a wonder that she and Anna had turned out to be reasonably normal, she thought, after that awful experience. God knows what would have happened to them if it weren't for Pete and his friend Mick.

TWELVE

DIDSBURY, MANCHESTER

September 1964

Pete glanced around the church hall that was filling up with teenagers in readiness for the Wednesday night youth club session. He looked across the room as he heard someone calling his name. Blonde-haired Mary Davies, Laura's friend from college, was waving her arm in the air and hurrying towards him. He stood up to greet her and gave her a hug. She looked pale and a bit anxious, and she glanced all around her before delving into her handbag and thrusting something at him.

'Let's go and sit over there where it's quiet before you look at that,' she told him, grabbing his arm and leading him to an empty table at the back of the room.

He pulled out two chairs and they sat down. He stared at the envelope in his hand, his eyes opening wide. It had Mary's address written on it, but it was in Laura's handwriting. 'When did you get this?' he asked, almost choking on his words.

'It came yesterday morning but I don't have your address. Laura wrote to me and said you would probably be here tonight, but that if you weren't, I had to tell any of your friends I could to call you at home as soon as possible to let you know you should get in touch with me. I haven't read the letter, but she's given me a brief explanation of where she is and she said you'd tell me more if you wanted to. I guess it saved her the time of writing things out twice.'

Pete took a deep breath and with shaking hands pulled the single sheet of paper from the envelope. He looked at Mary, his eyes filling, before opening it up, and she patted his hand. 'Read it, Pete,' she encouraged him.

Seeing Laura's neat handwriting almost broke his heart and he let out a strangled sob as he focused on her words:

My darling Pete,

I really hope this letter finds you, via Mary. I'm not allowed to write to you or call you in the normal way so this will have to do for now, I'm afraid. My mother has sent me away to a mother-and-baby home in Bollington, Cheshire. The name of the home is The Pines and it's on Dumbah Lane. She told me I cannot come home until I've had our baby and it's been adopted. I can't stay here, Pete, it's awful. The nuns are horrible and they treat us like slaves. I don't want our baby to be adopted, I want to keep it.

Will you please try and get me out of here? I miss you so much. I was ready and waiting at home for you with my case packed when my Uncle Ted came and took me to his house before you arrived to collect me. They wouldn't allow me to call you either. You can't write back to me here, but my friend Lydia will post on any letters you send to her at the address below. Please, please do your best to come for me. I'm scared and I love and miss you so much.

All my love, Laura Xxx

Tears running down his cheeks, Pete folded the letter and slipped it into his jacket pocket. He took a deep breath and wiped his eyes on the hanky Mary handed to him. His old friend Mick was waving to him across the room and Pete signalled for him to join them.

Mick hurried over and frowned. 'What's happened?' he asked and looked at Mary with a puzzled expression. 'You both look really upset.'

'This is Mary,' Pete introduced them. 'She's Laura's friend from college.'

'Nice to meet you, Mary,' Mick said and pulled out another chair. He sat down and looked closely at them both. 'Ah, I take it you've heard from Laura?' he said and they both nodded. 'So what's the score? Where is she?'

Pete took the letter from his pocket and handed it to Mick. 'Read it,' he said. 'I can't even bear to talk right now. The words would choke me.'

Mick silently read Laura's letter and shook his head. 'Oh, mate. I'm so bloody sorry. This is awful news. Poor Laura sounds desperate. Right, we've gotta try and get her out of there, and the sooner the better.'

Pete nodded. 'I need to write back to her at the friend's address she's given me but that's all going to take time. It won't be delivered in Buxton until Friday and then the friend has to forward it on to her. It could be next week before she knows that I'm aware of where she is – if they even let her have the letter.'

Mick chewed his lip, deep in thought. 'And you'll need somewhere to bring her to when we get her out of there. Right, I know you're having a hard time at home right now with your folks over this so do what I suggested the other night: leave home and move into the student house I share. There's a spare room you can have and it's much closer to work for you. Laura can move in with you when we get her.

It's better than nothing for now. The future can be sorted out another time.'

Pete took a deep breath and nodded. 'I'll do it. I'll go home now, write my letter to Laura and pack my stuff. Are you working tomorrow?'

Mick shook his head. 'I'm off tomorrow and Friday as I'm working the weekend this week. What I was going to suggest is that if you can take Friday off, we can ride up to Bollington on our scooters. We'll find the place easy enough and we can just keep riding up and down the lane until we get told to clear off by neighbours. With a bit of luck, Laura will see us riding past and realise that at least you now know where she is. I doubt they'll let us in – although there's no reason why we shouldn't knock at the door too.'

Mary and Pete both smiled at Mick's suggestion. 'That's a great idea,' Pete said. 'I'll take both days off with you and phone in sick. I can't face work at the moment with this on my mind anyway. I can move my stuff over tomorrow and then we can plan Friday properly. As long as Laura knows we're trying to sort things, now we know where she is, it will give her something to hold on to.'

At nine thirty on Friday morning, six parka-clad Mod friends of Pete and Mick's, sitting astride brightly coloured scooters covered in mirrors and fur, were assembled and waiting in St Bernadette's car park as Pete and Mick rode up to meet them. Last night, Mick had called a meeting at the shared student house and various friends had turned up. The ones who could get the day off work or college were willing to ride in a posse up to Bollington to attract attention in the hopes that Laura would see them or at least be made aware they were there. Pete was hoping she would put two and two together until his letter, via Lydia, hopefully reached her.

They had made a banner from an old white sheet and painted letters in red poster paint to say *Hang in There, Girl. The Mods Are Coming.* Mick suggested they didn't include her or Pete's names on the banner in case it got Laura into trouble with the nuns. They didn't wish to make her life any harder. This way they could wave the banner in the hope she would see it and read it and know it was for her. Pete had agreed it was the best they could do for now without getting them reported to the police for causing an affray in the village. And the nuns would be none the wiser which girl the message was meant for.

Pete's plan was to do this today and then tomorrow he was going to pay her witch of a mother a visit. See what she had to say when he told her he knew where Laura was being hidden and that he was going to get her out of there, and they'd have nothing more to do with her from that day on.

Mick took charge. 'Right, lads, thanks for coming, you know Pete really appreciates it. Now the plan is we'll get up to Bollington and find this Dumbah Lane place and then locate the house called The Pines. When we get outside there I want you to rev your scooters and make as much noise as you can to attract attention. We can then sing their song, right Pete? "Be My Baby" by the Ronettes. Hopefully, the nuns will all flock to the gates to see what's going on and that may mean the girls will have the freedom to look as well, then we wave the banner. Laura will recognise Pete's red scooter, I'm sure. And she knows that's their song. And hopefully, it will dawn on her that it's us lot, there for her. I doubt very much we'll get access to the house or we could bring her back with us, but we don't want to risk the police getting involved as they'd stop us and then God knows where she'd end up. Do you all understand?'

There was a general murmur of 'We do's' and Pete waved his thanks, feeling overcome. 'I'll treat you all to a pint tonight,' he managed to say, to cheers of agreement.

'Right then, let's go,' Mick said.

THIRTEEN

BOLLINGTON, CHESHIRE

September 1964

Laura and Anna linked arms with Barbara as the three of them strolled around the back garden, taking their Friday mid-morning exercise, thankful that the weekend was almost here and the daily chores would be lessened for a couple of days. Also, they were allowed to watch the TV on Saturday and Sunday evenings in the lounge from seven until ten o'clock, instead of sitting in their bedroom for hours on end. Two days ago, Barbara had received a birthday card, almost a week early, from Lydia, posted in Buxton.

Inside the card were two slips of paper, one each for Anna and Laura. Two simple words were written on both slips. *Mission accomplished* followed by a row of kisses. The card hadn't been opened or tampered with as far as they could tell, so that was good. And now Laura and Anna at least knew that their letters had been posted on to Pete, and to Tony's family. It was hopefully just a matter of time now, Laura thought.

As they made their way up the path towards the back porch

entrance, Barbara stopped walking and held a finger to her lips. 'What's that noise?' she asked, frowning.

Laura shook her head. 'Not sure, but if I didn't know better I'd say it sounds like motors revving up. Oh, maybe it's the gardeners.'

'They came on Tuesday,' Anna said. 'They won't be coming again this week.' She walked to the end of the path and popped her head round the side of the house. 'Oh, God, come here quick!' She beckoned to Laura and Barbara, who hurried to her side.

The revving noise was much louder here as the house wasn't blocking out the sound. The sight of four of the nuns hurrying down the sloping garden to the front gates, navy-blue gowns flapping behind them, stopped them from going any further, but they could see arms being waved in anger and fingers pointing at something going on in the lane just below. Horns tooted and several male voices began singing.

'Ooh, listen, they're singing that lovely Ronettes' song,' Barbara said, smiling. 'I love it, but who the devil can it be, and why are they here?'

One of the nuns shouted above the noise that she was going back to the house to call the police if the men didn't clear off immediately. Some of the girls were now on their way to where the nuns were standing, ignoring their angry glares and singing along. Laura's heart leapt as she realised the revving noise was coming from a gang of scooters parked up on the lane. She turned to Anna and Barbara, a big smile lighting up her pale face. The song was the one she and Pete had had their first dance to at the youth club; 'Be My Baby' had been theirs ever since.

'It's definitely lads on scooters,' she said. 'I can't see properly from up here but I think it may be the Didsbury Mods, which means my Pete will be with them. He must have got my letter.'

'Oh my goodness,' Anna said. 'Do you think so?'

Laura nodded. 'It could be. I'm going to go down near the gate, to get a closer look.' As she said that, Sister Ursula ran down the lawn and began pushing some of the girls back towards the front door, yelling at them to get moving.

'She's being a bit rough, isn't she?' Barbara said. 'She's just pushed poor Carol flying and now she's whacking her on the back. We'd better go and help her, quickly before she hurts her.' Barbara waddled away down the garden and shouted at Sister Ursula to stop.

Carol, whose baby was due next week, was on the ground screaming for help as Barbara came up behind the nun and shoved her to one side as hard as she could. 'Leave her alone, you bullying old cow,' she shouted as Sister Ursula turned towards her, hand raised. 'Just you try it,' Barbara warned, and watched as the nun's hand fell to her side, fist clenching and unclenching.

Carol screamed and clutched at her stomach. 'Oh my God, my waters have just broken. That's your fault.' She pointed at Sister Ursula, whose face was a seething mask of fury. The angry nun ran back into the house as Sister Celia and Sister Benedict came over to see what was going on. The two nuns still by the gate turned round also and, as they did so, Laura managed to sneak further down the lawn, until she could see the faces of the boys on the scooters through the metal railings on the gate.

She immediately spotted Pete's shiny red Lambretta with him sitting astride it and they made eye contact. He grinned and lifted his arm and she could see that he was holding one end of a banner, and then she saw Mick holding the other end. She read the banner's red lettering *Hang in There, Girl. The Mods Are Coming* as clanging bells sounded on the lane and two police panda cars came into view.

She was aware of Anna by her side, pulling on her arm. 'That's Pete?'

Laura nodded as a policeman jumped out of the passenger seat of one of the cars and grabbed hold of Pete's arm. He started to lead him away towards a police car, but not before Pete turned towards her and yelled, 'I'll be back as soon as I can. I love you. Don't let them take our baby away, don't sign anything.'

'I won't, and I love you too,' she mouthed. Tears poured down her cheeks as he was led away.

Anna put her arms round Laura. 'I'm so sorry. He's not done anything wrong really, so they won't charge him with much. I mean, singing and a bit of noise is hardly a crime. They've got hold of his friend too. Maybe they'll tell the police what a horrible place this is and they'll help get us out of here.'

Laura sighed. 'Even if they do, they probably won't believe them, so I won't be holding my breath.' She watched as Mick was also led towards a police car. Anna linked her arm and they walked back up the path to where poor Carol was howling in pain as three nuns tried to support her and bundle her back towards the house. 'Oh, no! I hope she'll be okay.'

Sister Ursula was now back outside, standing next to Barbara, an angry look on her face. She turned as Anna and Laura approached. 'Did that fiasco down there have anything to do with you two?' she barked.

'Of course not,' Anna replied, a look of innocence on her face. 'We just wanted to see what on earth was going on. We heard the noise of the engines, that's all. Was it you that called the police, Sister?'

'That's not your business to know, girl. Right, you can all get back inside now and you can forgo your lunch as a punishment. Any duties you were involved with today, you can now finish tomorrow.'

'Punishment? For what exactly?' Barbara protested. 'We're pregnant, we need to eat regularly. And tomorrow is Saturday; we only do light duties at the weekend.'

'You should have thought about that before you went gawping over the gate at those out-of-control young men. No wonder you're all in the mess you're in. Now get inside.' Sister Ursula marched on ahead as Barbara stuck two fingers in the air behind her back.

'Miserable old bitch,' Barbara yelled after her. 'I hope the police pay you a visit later. It's no more than you deserve after what you just did to Carol. And we're all witnesses to that.'

The nun's back stiffened but she carried on into the house without further retaliation. 'Hit a sore point there, I think,' Barbara said. 'I wonder what else she's got to hide.'

At a slight knocking noise, Laura put down the book she was reading and went to open the door. Olive Greaves was standing in the corridor, holding a loaded tray and looking nervously over her shoulder. Laura invited her in.

'Shut the door quick before they see me,' Olive said. 'I've brought you a brew and some sandwiches. I heard about what happened earlier when the nuns were talking while I served them their lunch,' she explained. 'They're all in a meeting now so I took my chance. You can't be without food and drink in your condition, it's not right.'

'Miss Greaves, you are an absolute angel,' Anna said, jumping off her bed and helping to clear a space on a dressing table top for the tray. 'We're spitting feathers and starving.'

Olive's cheeks flushed at the unexpected praise and she nodded. 'Thank you. And I'm not surprised. One of the girls has gone into labour and they've left her on her own up there.' She raised her eyes to the ceiling, indicating the delivery rooms on the floor above. 'It's not right. She should have the midwife nun with her. She's screaming. I just heard her as I came up the stairs.'

Barbara shook her head. 'That's poor Carol, Sister Ursula pushed her over in the garden earlier and her waters broke.'

Olive sighed. 'Oh, that's cruel, that's what it is—' She stopped and looked down, away from Barbara's gaze, in her usual shy manner. After a few seconds she glanced back up again and muttered, 'I'd better go or them nuns will have it in for me again.' She dashed out of the room and Barbara closed the door.

'I got the feeling Olive was about to say something else then, did you?' Barbara turned to Laura and Anna, who both nodded. 'Do you think something bad has happened to her here?'

'Yes,' Laura agreed. 'I do. Obviously, something to do with the baby she lost. She never speaks of it – well, she hardly speaks at all, except to us now. It's so good of her to take the risk of feeding us as well.'

'Poor Olive,' Anna said. 'I hope she's starting to think of us as friends. Maybe she'll confide in us as time goes on.'

'Who knows?' Laura sighed. 'Do you think we should go and see if Carol's okay? I can't believe they've left her on her own. Surely that's dangerous?'

Barbara shrugged and chewed her lip. 'Let's get this food eaten and then I'll slip up there on my own. There's no point in all of us getting into bother. I haven't got too much longer in here left anyway but you two have got until December, unless you get the help to escape before then. You don't want to be in the nuns' bad books for the rest of your stay.'

FOURTEEN

DIDSBURY, MANCHESTER

September 1964

Pete drank the last of his coffee, put his empty mug in the sink and slipped his long black leather coat on over a freshly ironed white shirt and slightly flared grey trousers. He picked up his Lambretta keys and went outside to start the scooter. At least it was a nice day today and he could arrive at his destination looking smart, rather than in his preferred casual jeans, black polo-neck sweater, topped with his parka.

First, he was going to pick up Mary, Laura's friend, who had suggested she come with him to Laura's mother's house. He felt glad of the offer of her company; thoughts of facing the miserable woman on his own after seeing Laura at The Pines yesterday made him feel sick. He had Laura's letter in his pocket and he was determined to make her mother read it and see what she was putting her daughter through when there was no need.

Not that she'd probably care, but still. It would make him feel he was doing as much as he could to get her home. Laura had looked pale and tired and it worried him. He still felt shaken from his almost-arrest yesterday, but when he'd explained to the policeman who interviewed him that all he was trying to do was get his girl out of the mother-and-baby home so that he could marry her, he'd been cautioned and advised to do things the correct way and talk to her parents to see if they would let her come home.

Fat chance, he thought, but at least they'd let him off and Mick too when he'd explained he was just trying to support his mate as all the lads were. Hopefully, the scooter boys had put the wind up the nuns, anyway. They might be worried they'd all turn up again and cause trouble. Maybe they'd treat the girls better now the address of The Pines was no longer a secret.

Mary was waiting at the front gate of her home for him and she waved as he pulled up. She climbed onto the pillion seat and told him to park up round the corner from Laura's home. 'It might be better if I go and knock on the door first and tell her I'm worried that Laura hasn't been to college for weeks and I'm concerned I haven't heard from her. See what excuses she comes up with.'

'Okay,' Pete agreed. 'If you think that's a good plan then we'll go for it.'

Mary nodded. 'I'll signal to you when I want you to casually stroll towards the house. Then we'll give it to her that we know where Laura is. We'll also tell her that you've spoken to the police. She doesn't need to know about them almost arresting you. We'll play up what they said a bit – if she doesn't slam the door in our faces, that is.'

Pete parked the scooter round the corner from Laura's home as Mary had instructed. She climbed off the back seat and hurriedly tidied her long hair with a small brush she took out of her shoulder bag. She tucked the side lengths behind her ears, straightened her black skirt and jacket and smiled. 'Right, do I look like I mean business?'

Pete smiled and nodded. 'Well, I wouldn't like to cross you.'

'Wish me luck, then. You can see me from here, but she won't be able to spot you if you keep behind this big tree. I'll raise my hand when I need you to join me. Did you notice as we came past that there's a big posh car on the drive and also one parked on the road outside the gate? She must have visitors, so she might just see me off as soon as I mention Laura's name. We shall see.'

Mary strolled confidently up the road and onto the drive of Laura's family home. She raised an eyebrow at the large Jaguar car that was parked on the drive. As she stood on the doorstep, she could hear muffled male and female voices coming from inside the house and cocked an ear but couldn't make out what anyone was saying. There was a choice of a doorbell or a well-polished brass knocker on the bottle-green-painted front door. Mary chose the bell and stood back to wait.

'Ted, will you get that door?' a female voice said as the door was opened by a tall grey-haired man, who smiled at Mary. He looked beyond her as though expecting her to be accompanied.

'Good morning, Miss. Erm, are you from Slater and Green's?' he asked.

'Who?' Mary frowned, taking a step backwards. 'I've come to speak to Mrs Sims if she's at home, please.'

'Oh, right. Well, if you'll just wait a minute, love. Lillian!' the man called over his shoulder. 'Think you need to speak with this young lady here, she's asking for your sister.'

A plump woman with neatly set grey hair appeared beside him, her eyes red-rimmed as though she'd been crying. She dabbed at her nose with a handkerchief and stared at Mary. 'You asked for my sister? So you're not from the funeral directors then? Only we're expecting them later today.'

Mary shook her head, feeling puzzled. 'No, I'm a friend of

Laura's from college and I've come on behalf of all her friends as we are concerned that she's not been to college for a while, she's not been in touch with me and no one has seen her. Why do you think I'm from the funeral directors? Has someone died?'

The woman called Lillian spoke. 'You'd better come inside quick before the neighbours see you.' She grabbed Mary by the arm and bundled her inside, and the man closed the door. 'Follow me,' the woman instructed and led the way into a room at the front of the house, where the curtains were closed. 'Please sit down.' She pointed to a chair set in the bay window alcove.

Mary did as she was told and stared at the woman, who looked worried.

'I'm afraid my niece isn't here right now,' the woman began, stumbling over her words. 'She's, erm, she's been sent away to a private college near London to study.'

Mary raised her eyebrows. 'Your niece? Ah, then you must be Aunty Lil. I've heard Laura mention you and her Uncle Ted,' she said. 'She's been sent to a private college, you say? How very odd that Laura never mentioned it to me and I'm her best friend at Hollings College. She just vanished overnight. I get a feeling that something isn't right here. Why did you ask if I was from the undertakers?' she directed at Laura's uncle, who was hovering by the door, a worried expression on his face.

'Oh, nothing to worry about there,' he said quickly. 'Laura's fine. It's her mother we need the undertakers for. I'm afraid she passed away suddenly yesterday.'

Mary gaped at him. 'Really? How, I mean, was it an accident or something?'

'No, not an accident,' Lillian answered. 'My sister sadly passed in her sleep. They are doing a post-mortem today. We need a death certificate for the undertaker, that's why Ted thought you'd come to collect it – but of course we haven't got it yet, it's a bit too early for them to have finished.'

'I see.' Mary nodded thoughtfully. 'I'm so sorry to hear that. So I guess Laura is on her way home by train? She'll be so upset. It's not that long since she lost her father but it will be good to see her again.'

'Erm, no, there's no need for her to come home. We'll see to everything here,' Lillian said hurriedly. 'The, erm, college won't let her have the time off as she's studying for a very important exam.'

Mary snorted. 'Stop right there! No time off for her own mother's funeral? That's ridiculous.' She looked up as two more people crowded into the room, a man and a woman. Much younger than Ted and Lillian, but they had similar features.

'Our son and daughter, Laura's cousins,' Lillian said by way of introduction. 'They've come home from their respective universities to help us organise their aunt's funeral.'

'So *they've* managed to get out of uni but Laura can't get time off from this so-called private college?' Mary said. 'Hang on there for a minute.' She jumped up and went to the front door, opened it and stood on the drive, waving in Pete's direction.

He hurried towards her and she led him into the lounge, where the family were now huddled together, all talking at once. They stopped as Mary and Pete stood in the doorway.

'Right.' Mary took charge of the conversation. 'This is Pete, in case you've never met him before. And this' – she turned to Pete – 'is Laura's aunt and uncle and her cousins, their son and daughter.'

Pete nodded in the family's direction and Mary continued. She told him of their misconception in thinking she was from the funeral directors. His eyebrows rose as she continued: 'Laura's mother has apparently passed away and a post-mortem is being conducted as we speak. However, they tell me that Laura is away at a private college in London that she's unable to get leave from to attend her own mother's funeral. But their kids have got uni leave to attend. All a bit weird, don't you think, Pete?'

He took a deep breath. 'Very weird, Mary, considering I saw Laura only yesterday in the garden of a mother-and-baby home in Bollington village in Cheshire.'

'You did what?!' Lillian exclaimed as her son and daughter stared at her in bewilderment, leaving Mary to assume they knew nothing of their cousin's current predicament.

'You heard,' Pete told her. 'I saw Laura yesterday,' he repeated. 'Ah, in case you don't know, Laura is expecting my baby and we want to get married. Instead, she was sent away without my knowledge by her mother and these two here,' he told the cousins, who looked aghast.

As Lillian sat down heavily on the sofa and put her head in her hands, Pete told Laura's cousins exactly what had happened in July and then took the letter from his pocket and gave it to the girl, who introduced herself as Felicity and her brother as Harry. Tears poured down Felicity's cheeks as she read her cousin's heartfelt words. Ted sat with his arm round his wife as she sobbed.

'Mum,' Felicity said, 'how could you have been a part of this-this awful act? It's the sixties and times are moving on. Surely Aunty Audrey wasn't bothered about what her snobby neighbours would think? This is just so cruel. Laura sounds heartbroken and at the end of her tether in this letter.'

'She is,' Pete said. 'We want to get married but your aunt said we couldn't. When I came to get Laura next day to run away to Gretna Green with her, she'd already been sent away to your parents' place, as she says there in her letter. I had no idea how to contact her or even where she was. It's been a nightmare. And now we have this mystery college story.'

'So-so Laura's not at college? And she's been sent to this place?' Harry said, clearly trying to get his head around everything.

Mary and Peter both nodded vigorously. 'Has her mother really died or is that another lie? And does Laura know?' Pete asked.

Ted looked up from his place on the sofa and shook his head. 'It's true, our Audrey passed away yesterday,' he confirmed. 'You may as well know that we have reason to believe she took her own life. She suffered from mental health problems in the past that have come home to roost since Jack died last year – that's Laura's father. And now with the problems she's had with Laura recently, we think it's tipped her over the edge.'

Mary shook her head. 'There wouldn't have been any need to send Laura away if her mother had listened to what she and Pete wanted and stopped worrying about what the narrow-minded neighbours would think. Pete and I came here today to try and persuade Audrey to let Laura come home and marry him.'

Lillian got to her feet. 'Yes, well, Audrey couldn't handle the shame of it. I think you should go now. Laura doesn't know about her mother's death yet. We will let the nuns at The Pines know in time and they can break it to her as gently as possible. But we are her legal guardians now until she's twenty-one and we will decide on what's best for her. We'll respect her mother's wishes – it's the least we can do. There's no need for her to attend the funeral, as we'll tell everyone that she's been delayed in London for the foreseeable future. We have a lot to deal with here, as you can imagine.'

Pete narrowed his eyes. 'You're not letting Laura come to her own mother's funeral? And surely she should have some say in things? This house will be hers. It shouldn't be down to you to make all the decisions on her behalf. And no way is she staying in that appalling home if it's anything to do with me.'

'Well, it isn't, is it, young man?' Lillian said. 'This is a family affair. We are now Laura's guardians and we will make the decisions for her. Now I think you should leave.'

'Mum, I can't believe what you've just said to Pete,' Felicity snapped. 'Who the hell do you think you are? You're turning into Aunty Audrey, for goodness' sake. My God, I've got to get out of here before I say or do something I'll regret.'

'Felicity, please. Don't make a scene,' Lillian tried to shout over her.

'No, I'm done. You can sort this mess out yourself and I will not be going to the funeral after the way she's treated Laura. But I tell you this, I will stand by my cousin and Pete.'

Felicity turned to her brother, who had remained silent, but white-faced, throughout all the shouting. She took a deep breath and spoke more quietly: 'Harry, are you with me on this one?' Harry nodded his agreement as she continued. 'Aunty Audrey never liked us anyway. In fact, she didn't like kids, full stop. She said so often enough. I'm surprised that she even had Laura. She hated Uncle Jack too; you could see it in her eyes. She always looked at him like he was shit on her shoe. I don't know why a nice man like him ever married a cold fish like her. And, Pete, tell Laura we'll take her cat Sooty with us and I'll keep him in my room at uni until she's ready to have him back.'

'Thank you,' Pete said. 'She'll appreciate that, I'm sure. Write your address down for me and I'll let you know how things go. I'll let Laura know that I've spoken to you and maybe you could drop her a line now and again.'

Felicity nodded. 'I'll be glad to.' She grabbed a pad and pen from the coffee table and hurriedly scribbled down her university address. 'Take care, and give Laura mine and Harry's love, if and when you see her. She knows me better as Fliss,' she added, handing the notepad page to Pete. She glared at her parents and shook her head. 'How you can even think this is okay, I don't know but it's not something I can ever forgive you for.' She slammed the door as she left the room and followed Pete and Mary down the hall to the front door.

'I'm so sorry about all this,' she apologised to Pete. 'Mum was always falling out with Aunty Audrey, but seemed to take her side when she shouldn't. Well, there's no way I can go to the funeral now and cry crocodile tears over someone who never liked me in the first place. Not after the way she's treated our Laura.'

'I understand,' Pete said. 'I'd feel the same. I wish I could be there for Laura when the nuns give her the news.'

Felicity gave him a hug. 'One day this will all be behind you and then you and Laura can move on. I wish you well. And, Mary, thanks for being there for both of them. Laura's lucky to have a friend like you.'

June 2015

Laura and Pete were waiting for a call from Inspector Jackson. He was coming to see them and to collect the statements that she and Anna had made, containing as many details as they could remember from their time at The Pines. A television and newspaper appeal had gone out recently, asking for information from anyone who had been resident at The Pines during certain dates, or knew anyone who was.

Confirmation was now available that all the skeletons found in the gardens belonged to small mammals and animals; no human remains were amongst them. Anna wasn't alone in thinking that her babies had been sold, so an investigation into illegal baby trafficking was now under way.

Laura's cousin Fliss, who was now a solicitor with a Manchester law firm, was coming to visit that evening and staying for a few nights. She'd told Laura and Pete during a phone call the previous day that she'd been following the reports about The Pines and would like to have a chat about them, as it might now open up new possibilities in their search for Paul. She also said she had something for Laura that she had discovered in the loft of her late parents' house. She'd found it when she and her brother Harry had been clearing it out, prior to putting the property on the market.

'Let's have a quick coffee before we get swamped by visitors,' Laura suggested. Anna and Mick were also on their way over, so the day would no doubt be busy. As she stood in the kitchen waiting for the kettle to boil, Laura wondered what the discovery might be. She hadn't seen her aunt and uncle for years; after they'd been complicit in sending her away while she was pregnant, she'd never been able to forgive them.

Maybe it was something left over from when they'd cleared out Laura's mother's house following her death, while Laura was still in The Pines, and they'd forgotten to give it to her. She hoped it was something nice to do with her beloved dad. Maybe photographs, as she had so few of him and she knew that a lot had been taken when she was a child with his Box Brownie camera. It was a mystery what had happened to them all. She could live in hope. She heard the phone ringing again and Pete answered it as she made two quick mugs of coffee and carried them into the lounge.

Pete followed her and sat down beside her on the sofa. 'That was Inspector Jackson, they're fifteen minutes away, so hopefully, Mick and Anna will be here soon too. Shall we eat out tonight when your Fliss arrives? Saves us cooking and I'm sure she won't mind. We can go to that Italian we keep saying we'll try, Amo Trattoria. I've heard it's really good.'

Laura smiled and nodded. 'Sounds like a good idea to me.'

'Oh well, you know me, I'm full of 'em,' Pete quipped. 'I suppose I'd better call my mother later this week as well. I've not spoken to her since her birthday last month. Mind you, the phone works two ways. She could just as easily ring me occasionally.' He picked up his mug and took a mouthful of coffee.

'Yes, you should,' Laura agreed. Pete's mum Angie, who was

now in her late eighties, had been widowed the previous year and she often said how lonely she felt at times. 'She could always get the train to Lime Street and come and stay for a few days if she feels up to it? Or we could even go down and get her. I think she's a bit embarrassed since The Pines news broke.'

'Yes, I agree. I think she still blames herself for her part in us not being able to get married when we first wanted to,' said Pete.

'But it was all *my* mum's fault for being so horrible to her. It hurt Angie's feelings, so she lashed out the only way she knew how – and that was to stop you from marrying me so my mother would be ashamed and embarrassed in front of her stuck-up neighbours with an unmarried teenage mother on her hands. Once Mum started the ball rolling, there was no stopping it, and by the time your mum changed her mind it was all too late, I'd been shipped out of town,' said Laura.

'You're right, but I don't think she's ever forgiven herself for us losing Paul. After all, he was her first and only grandson.' All three of Pete's younger brothers were fathers to daughters as Pete now was.

'Like us, she would have been so very proud of him,' Laura said sadly. 'Anyway, she's not seen her great-grandees for a while, so she'll enjoy that. Maybe we could go and pick her up and bring her over, although I know she always says she likes to do the train ride. She worries me at times with the way she insists on being so independent for her age and tells us off for treating her like an old woman!'

Pete smiled and shook his head.

'Invite her over and we'll work out the logistics of the journey if she says yes. Maybe the girls could go and pick her up. We'll sort something out. Ah—' She stopped talking, her ear cocked. 'Doorbell. Go and let in whoever it is and I'll re-boil the kettle. That's all we ever seem to do lately – brew up, answer the door and the flippin' phone.'

'True,' Pete called over his shoulder as he went to let in the policemen and Anna and Mick, who'd arrived at the same time.

Inspector Jackson smiled as Laura handed him a mug of coffee. 'I wish all our visits were as pleasant as the ones we make to you,' he said. 'We feel really looked after when we come here.' He reached for a chocolate digestive biscuit from a plate Laura had placed on the coffee table. 'Luxury,' he said, admiring it, as Laura laughed.

'Well, you've driven a fair way to be here and it's the least we can do,' she said, smiling.

He nodded. 'I know we could pass the visit over to a local station who would send a couple of officers to see you with the same details we have, but this case isn't like anything we've dealt with before. I want to see it through to the end.' He finished his refreshments and then got down to the business in hand.

'Well, after Anna's claims that her twins were sold and with the lack of paperwork to go on, as you know, we put out a local appeal. We've had a couple of people coming forward in confidence with a few interesting stories. Most of them have lived in the village pretty much all of their lives and one of them is the chap who alerted us to the first lot of remains. He's the on-site gardener at the moment.'

The inspector took a sip of coffee and continued. 'He remembers when he was a young lad, his mother and aunties sitting in the kitchen, gossiping about The Pines, which he'd heard tell was a home for wayward girls. Not a very nice title, I admit, and I'm sorry, ladies, they're his words not mine.'

He smiled sadly at Laura and Anna, who smiled back. 'Anyway, even though his mum used to shoo him out of the room, he still managed to hide behind the door and overheard various conversations. He overheard rumours of dead babies and how they were buried in the garden, which his mum and the aunts thought was very wrong, but they didn't do anything about it. I think they were all a bit in awe of the nuns and you didn't tell tales on religious orders in those days. But of course it backs up the story of what the nuns used to tell the girls when a child had supposedly died at birth.

'The other person who came forward was a lady who told us she gave birth to a stillborn baby at The Pines in 1960. She was a bit older than most of the girls who were sent to the home. She says she ended up with some mental health problems and a spell in a psychiatric hospital and then because she had no home to go back to, the nuns allowed her to return to them. They made her work very hard for her keep. Her name is Olive, but we are keeping her surname private as she's frightened. The nuns always warned her that if she told tales on them, she would be struck down by God. Poor soul has been religiously brainwashed, it would seem. She was terrified of speaking to us at first, but she has a lot of information and although she seems a bit confused at times about present-day things, she's got a good recall of the past. It was very brave of her to come forward.'

'Oh my goodness, that's Olive,' Laura said, feeling overcome. 'We do know her, very well. She was so sweet and shy but treated horribly by the nuns. They kept her almost like a slave.'

Anna nodded, her eyes filling with tears. 'Olive really looked after me the weeks before my twins were born and she saw a lot that went on in there. So many times she started to tell us things, but always scuttled away before she finished in case a nun was listening in to our conversations. We did get a fair bit out of her at times though; she trusted us.'

'So you remember her?' Inspector Jackson said. 'Well, that's good news because I would like to arrange a meeting for you both with Olive, if that's alright with you. I think with your help she may feel more relaxed and able to talk freely without the fear of thinking she's being eavesdropped on.'

'That would be lovely,' Laura said. 'I tell you what, why not bring her here? She may feel more comfortable than if we were to meet in an office at the police station or something, and also, if she's away from the village, she'll know no one is listening in on the conversations. Would it be possible to do that?'

'Leave it with me,' Inspector Jackson said. 'It will be much better and far more informal, and we will tell her she's going to meet up with two old friends again who are really looking forward to seeing her. As soon as I can get a date set, I'll be in touch. We'll bring her over in an unmarked police car and then she won't feel embarrassed when we go to pick her up, like she's been arrested or something. I really do feel that Olive is our best witness to date, with probably an awful lot more to tell us than she already has done.'

Laura smiled. 'Yes, that sounds great. I'll even bake a cake – Olive always made nice ones for us. It's time for us to treat her.'

'Then we'll definitely have our meeting here,' Inspector Jackson said with a smile. 'One way or another, we will get to the bottom of this appalling mess and hopefully, we may be able to tell you what happened to your missing children.'

'That would be wonderful,' Laura said. 'I need to ask you something before you go.' She went on to tell him of their daughters' suggestion that they start a Facebook group for The Pines to reunite families separated by the mother-and-baby home.

He nodded slowly. 'I can't see that it will do any harm. It may well bring more people forward with further information. What we do know so far is that all the nuns who were living and working there are no longer with us and neither are the priests of the Catholic church in the near vicinity. All we can rely on now is getting our information from members of the public, like yourselves, who were involved during that time.

What we're looking for is the people who provided the false birth certificates and any paperwork that was given to the adoptive families. Because as sure as hell, anything written on it was false information. But again, it's all so long ago that finding anyone still alive, apart from all you parents who were so young back then, isn't going to be an easy task.'

SIXTEEN

BOLLINGTON, CHESHIRE

September 1964

Laura and Anna had just come indoors from their stroll around the gardens when they were met by a worried-looking Olive, who told Laura that Sister Celia wanted to see her in the office right away.

Laura rolled her eyes. 'Ye gods, what have I done now?' she asked. Olive shrugged in response and shook her head. 'Won't be a minute,' Laura said and hurried towards the office.

Anna and Olive stared after her and then Olive dug into her apron pocket and pushed a crumpled envelope addressed to Barbara into Anna's hand. 'Pass this on for me,' she said quietly, placing a finger to her lips. She took a quick look over her shoulder to check they were still alone and whispered, 'And just to let you know, Carol's gone home this morning. A man in a car came for her.' She hurried away down the hall towards the kitchen.

Anna frowned, wishing they could at least have said goodbye to Carol after her awful ordeal. But, as they all knew, the nuns tried to prevent any contact after a girl had given birth.

Olive had already told them that poor Carol's baby was born dead and had been buried by the nuns in the garden. Hardly surprising after she'd been shoved around by Sister Ursula last week. They'd all heard her terrified screams that night and into the following day, until she finally went quiet. Anna hoped Carol would be okay and that her family would welcome her home.

She took another peek at the letter in her pocket and wondered why it hadn't been given directly to Barbara, but as she felt the thickness of it she realised it would most likely contain letters for her and Laura also. The postcode was a Buxton one, so was definitely sent from Lydia. It was first class and date-stamped the end of last week. This should have been delivered here on Tuesday at the latest, Anna thought as she pushed the envelope into her pocket. It was now Friday and a week since Pete and his friends had turned up on their scooters at the gates.

She'd bet her life the nuns had held on to it, with no intention of ever giving it to Barbara. They'd probably chucked it in the wastepaper bin. Thank God Olive cleaned the office and was responsible for bin-emptying duties. Anna walked slowly to the laundry room to resume the morning's tasks. Barbara was busy mangling sheets and she turned to smile at Anna and ran a hand across her sweaty brow.

'Laura not with you?'

'She's been summoned to Sister Celia's office,' Anna told her, raising an eyebrow.

'Really? Blimey, wonder what that's all about?'

'No idea. Olive came to find us as we came back inside from our walk.' Anna lowered her voice and indicated the envelope in her blue smock pocket. 'She gave me this,' she mouthed. 'It's addressed to you.'

Barbara stuck up a thumb and smiled. 'Great,' she whispered.

'Stop gossiping and get on with your work, you two,' Sister Ursula shouted across the room. 'You can miss your tea break if you haven't finished those sheets in five minutes.'

'Yes, Sister,' Barbara called back and then muttered under her breath, 'no sister, three bags bloody full, Sister.'

Swallowing nervously and hoping that she wasn't in any bother, Laura knocked on the door of Sister Celia's office and rocked back on the heels of her shoes, waiting for a response.

The door opened and Sister Celia beckoned her to come inside with a half-smile.

'Please be seated, Miss Sims.' The nun pointed to a hard wooden chair and plonked herself down on the opposite side of the large oak desk on a more comfortable and well-padded chair.

Laura did as she was told and looked at Sister Celia, who made a steeple of her fingers as she took a deep breath.

'I'm afraid I have taken a phone call this morning from your Aunt Lillian,' she began, a slightly sympathetic tone to her voice. 'I'm afraid I have some bad news for you. Sadly, I've been told that your dear mother passed away late last week.'

Laura gasped and shook her head. 'My mother? She's dead?'

'Yes, I'm afraid she passed away,' repeated Sister Celia.

Laura tried to take it in. 'She died last week and I'm only just being told this news? Why didn't you tell me immediately?' Her questions tumbled over one another. 'She wasn't ill, as far as I knew. I must go home.' She jumped to her feet. 'I'll need to organise a funeral. Where's the nearest train station to here?'

'Please sit back down, Miss Sims, and allow me to finish. The funeral is taking place today. Your aunt informs me that she and your uncle have dealt with everything. There is no need for you to go home. In fact, as I understand it, that would be against your late mother's wishes.'

'But she's my mum,' Laura protested, tears starting. 'She's dead. I should have been the one dealing with all this, not my aunt and uncle. I'm going home, whether you like it or not.'

Sister Celia got to her feet and hurried to the door, barring Laura's way. 'You are going nowhere,' she said firmly. 'The family do not want you to go home. Your aunt made that quite clear during our conversation.'

'You can't stop me and neither can they,' Laura yelled, pushing the nun out of the way as Sister Ursula burst into the room and grabbed Laura by the upper arms. 'Ouch, let go of me!' she screamed at the nun, who dug her bony fingers in.

'Calm down,' Sister Ursula said and pushed Laura back onto the chair she'd vacated.

'Calm down?' Laura said, a sob catching her throat as she rubbed her upper arms where the nun's sharp nails had made marks. 'How do you expect me to calm down when I've just been told my mother has passed away, her funeral is taking place right now and I'm not allowed to go home and see my family? What sort of heartless creature are you? Don't even bother answering that – I've seen how you treat the girls here. It's disgusting. As soon as I'm out of here I'll be reporting all of you to the authorities.'

'Shut up, right now,' Sister Ursula ordered. 'You are doing penance for your sins. It was your choice to give in to your disgusting carnal desires, you are now reaping what you sowed. All we are doing here is giving you a roof over your head when no one else will. We make sure you are fed and taken care of, and then we will find a loving home for the child you are obviously not capable of looking after yourself. There is *nothing* to report to anyone.'

She turned on her heel and left the room, slamming the door, leaving Laura with Sister Celia, who spoke quietly: 'Right, Miss Sims, I think we're quite finished here for now. Your aunt said to inform you she will be writing to you shortly. But you are to stay here in our care under her instructions and your late mother's wishes until after the birth and adoption of your baby. Then arrangements will be made for you to go home to stay with your relatives.'

Laura stared at Sister Celia. 'I'm not giving up my baby. I don't care what any of them, or you, say. I'm keeping it. My boyfriend will not allow our baby to be given away. We want to get married. I'm sick of repeating myself about this. I don't need to go home to them anyway. My dad always told me our house would be mine if anything happened to him and my mother. I have my own home now. I can go back there; I don't need to be here.'

Sister Celia shook her head, got to her feet and pointed to the door. 'You've had a shock and you're not thinking straight. You should go to your room now and rest until suppertime. Miss Greaves will bring you up a snack at lunchtime.'

Laura jumped up and ran to the door, yanking it open. There was no point in wasting any more breath here. No one was listening to her anyway. She hurried upstairs and flung herself onto her bed, tears running down her cheeks. But strangely enough they weren't for the loss of her mother, but for herself and her unborn baby. She folded her arms protectively round her neat bump and hugged it. 'I won't let anyone take you away,' she whispered. 'Daddy and I love you and want you so much, my baby. We'll make a home for you in our very own house.' She cried herself into a deep sleep and didn't even stir when Olive brought her a tray up a while later.

* * *

As soon as their chores were finished, Anna and Barbara hurried up to their shared bedroom to look for Laura. She hadn't been present at lunchtime and Olive had whispered that

Laura was in their bedroom, but she didn't elaborate further. They let themselves in just as Laura was waking up.

Anna sat down on the end of Laura's bed as she opened her eyes, looking puzzled momentarily. She sat up slowly and shook her head as Barbara pulled up a chair and sat down beside Anna. 'What's happened?' Anna asked. 'Why did Sister Celia want to see you? We've been worried to death when you didn't come back to the laundry and then you also missed lunch.' She indicated the tray that was still on the bedside table, the mug of tea, now cold with an unappetising milky skim on the surface, and the sandwiches curling at the edges. 'I see Olive looked after you, but you must have been asleep. What is it, Laura, what's happened?'

Laura took a deep breath and told them of her meeting with Sister Celia and what was said. She finished, 'So I am now officially an orphan.'

Barbara stared at her. 'And they won't let you go home for your mother's funeral? What sort of unfeeling monsters are they?'

Laura shrugged. 'The family don't want me there. They are too ashamed of me to even let me back home to see my mother buried. We were never that close, but she was still my mum at the end of the day and I should be there to say a final goodbye to her. Well, that's it. I wash my hands of the lot of them from now on.'

'And I don't blame you,' Anna said. 'I know you said you didn't get on with your mum and you found it hard to forgive her for sending you here, but even so, like you say, she *was* still your mother. They can't do this, it's simply not right.'

'Too late, Anna, it's already done and dusted as far as they're all concerned. Apart from Pete, I'm all alone in this world now.'

'Oh, talking of Pete...' Anna delved into her pocket and thrust the envelope she'd been carrying in Barbara's direction.

'Open it, quick; let's see what the witches were trying to keep from us.'

Barbara hurriedly ripped open the envelope and took out three letters, one for each of them. Barbara's was from Lydia; Anna's a reply from Tony's mum. And Laura's was from Pete. Laura and Anna each unfolded their sheets of paper with shaking hands.

Laura took a deep breath and tears rolled down her cheeks as she read Pete's heartfelt words:

My darling Laura,

I can't believe what your mother has done, sending you away. I went to get you as planned and she told me you'd gone and slammed the door in my face. Thank you for managing to get a letter to me via Mary. Mick and I are putting a plan into action and we will do our best to at least try and rescue you as soon as we can, and if that's not possible then we will just keep on trying.

I am leaving home and moving into Mick's shared house tomorrow, Thursday, so that you and I will at least have a room to ourselves when I can get you out of The Pines. Watch out for the scooter gang on Friday, though I doubt you will see this letter until after then. But we'll make a lot of noise to attract attention, so I hope you do see us and then you will know we are doing our best. At least I know where you are now, which is a relief.

If we can't rescue you as planned, then I am going to go and see your mother on Saturday to try again to persuade her to let you come home to me. Please try and be brave and I promise we'll be together again one day. Don't let them take our baby. It belongs with us, not strangers. Write to me again as soon as you can if you're not rescued by the time you read this. If it helps, send it to Mary's address rather than me putting Mick's on here and risk anyone finding it and confiscating the letter. I'll send this letter to your friend's address that you gave me and I hope it reaches you eventually. It's ridiculous that we have to do all this cloak-and-dagger stuff when all we want is to be together.

Anyway, whatever it takes. I love you with all my heart and I can't wait to see you again. Goodbye for now, my girl, all my love, Pete xxx

* * *

Anna swallowed hard as she read Tony's mum's letter. Her eyes filled and she shook her head sadly.

Dearest Anna,

As soon as we got your letter we went straight round to see your mum and dad to demand an explanation and to give them what-for. How dare they do this to you? Sending you away when you're expecting our Tony's baby; you should be with us. We're family and we will look after you both. I'm sure you already know that, love. We demanded they bring you home and we take you to ours. They refused. I told your mother she's got no heart and she told me to mind my own business.

Unfortunately, they will not agree to our suggestions and have told us that they will let the nuns know that, if we show up at The Pines making trouble, they are to inform the police right away and you will be moved to another home with immediate effect.

I don't know what else to do, love. I don't want to make things any harder for you than they already are. We're going to go and see a solicitor next week to see if we have any legal rights. That baby is our only connection to our dear lost son, our flesh and blood and our first grandchild. Just keep in touch

with us when you can and we will continue to try and get
some help if it's possible.

You now know that you have a home here with us and so
does your baby. Keeping that in mind may help you cope
better. Let's work on that for now. Sending you our best wishes
and letting you know we are thinking of you all the time. With
love from Dot and Frank (Tony's mam and dad)

Anna sighed and refolded her letter. Well, at least they
knew about the baby now and were being supportive. It was
good to know she had someone on her side who was willing to
help and look after her and the baby. All she had to do now was
get out of this place; easier said than done though.

She wondered if they'd seen the solicitor yet and what had
been said there. No doubt they'd tell her in their next letter.
She'd write to them after tea when they were free to relax up
here in their room, and then hopefully, Olive might be able to
get stamps and post them on her duty visits to the post office for
the nuns. She looked across to Laura, who was slumped on her
bed, looking miserable.

'Anything good to report?' Anna asked.

Laura shook her head. 'Not really. He told me they were
planning to come here on Friday on scooters, which we already
know about, and that he was going to see my mum on the Saturday. But, according to what Sister Celia told me, she was probably already dead by then. He's left home and got us a room we
can stay in at his mate Mick's place, so at least we will have a
roof over our heads, as and when I can escape from here. God,
it's all so hopeless.'

Laura burst into tears and Anna put an arm round her
shoulders. She told her and Barbara what Tony's mum had said.
'I don't hold out much hope, to be honest, but at least they are
there for me, which is good to know.'

Barbara joined in a group hug with them. 'Those are both

really good things, loves. You've got people who love you once we get you out of here,' she said.

'How's Lydia?' Laura asked. 'Is she coping back at work?'

'She seems to be. She says she often thinks about her baby and how it's doing, even though she knew she couldn't keep it. They never told her the sex, you know. Just whisked it away as soon as it was born and that was that. Two days in bed resting with none of us allowed up to see her and then packed off back home before she was fit to be discharged.'

'I find this whole thing really weird,' Laura said. 'The fact that we're not even allowed to know what sex the baby is, unless we happen to catch sight of it.' The others nodded their agreement. 'Do you think they drug the mothers in the final stages of labour so they don't have a clue what's going on?'

Barbara shrugged. 'It wouldn't surprise me. Maybe Olive would know.'

'Well, if she does, I doubt she'd tell us. She'd be too scared.' Laura sighed as the supper bell rang out. 'I suppose we'd better go and eat.'

'Oh, by the way,' Anna said, 'Olive told me that Carol went home today.'

'Poor Carol,' Barbara said, shaking her head. 'And that poor baby. It never stood a chance with the way they do things in here.'

SEVENTEEN

WEST DERBY, LIVERPOOL

June 2015

'Can I get you two a brew or maybe a G&T?' Pete asked as Laura and her cousin Fliss flopped down onto the sofa, sighing contentedly. The threesome had just arrived back from the Italian restaurant and Fliss had declared as they strolled home that she was stuffed to the gills. Laura had said that she was too. Three courses of rich Italian food and two bottles of wine was more than enough and, even though they'd walked instead of getting a taxi as planned, they laughingly agreed it would take a few more days to work off the rest of the calories.

'Perhaps just a teeny G&T,' Laura said, screwing up her face and indicating the size with her finger and thumb. 'I couldn't manage anything else, thanks, love. Fliss, are you joining me?'

Fliss puffed her cheeks out. 'Oh, go on then, if I must! Teeny for me too.' She grinned as Pete laughed and went into the kitchen.

He came back into the lounge with a small tray and three

filled glasses and handed the drinks out. He raised his in a toast: 'Good to see you again, Fliss. We should do this more often.'

'Indeed we should,' Fliss agreed. 'When I can get a day or two off work, that is. I know I should retire now at my age and maybe I will after Christmas. When the sale of the family home goes through and I can finally pay off my mortgage, I can take life a bit easier. You two did the right thing, retiring a few years ago. But I do enjoy my job and I've cut down the hours quite a bit. Before I finish for good though, and now we know things at The Pines were not what they seemed, I want to help you find your son. I'd also like to offer my assistance to anyone else who might be searching for lost children.'

'I'm sure Anna will be glad of all the help she can get,' Laura said. 'We're definitely going to start the search for our Paul again. We've asked the policeman who's helping us if it will be okay to set up a Facebook page and our girls are going to get us started this weekend. He said to go ahead – he can't see it doing any harm to their investigation.'

Fliss nodded. 'I've heard that a few Facebook groups set up for past mother-and-baby homes have been quite successful, so it's a good idea to get one up and running for The Pines. Social media is the way to go these days. I do feel, though, that because of the way it's looking like the babies were very likely stolen and illegally sold, it may not be as straightforward as some of the other groups are.'

'Do you think so?' asked Pete.

'Yes, the adopted children will have no legal birth certificates and may never even have been told that they were adopted. DNA checking is a good way, but if you have no clue that you are not the child of the people who brought you up, then you won't be looking. All we can hope for is that something will have triggered a thought or maybe a feeling somehow they don't belong, like a square peg in a round hole. It's in the lap of the gods – but if we don't try, we'll never know.'

Fliss swallowed her drink in one go and put the glass down on the coffee table. 'Would you two mind if I go up to bed? I was up so early today, I'm struggling to keep my eyes open.'

'You go ahead,' Pete said as Laura nodded her agreement. 'We won't be far behind you. Your case is in your room and you know where the bathroom is. We'll see you in the morning for a full English. That'll help the hangover you're bound to wake up with.'

'I hope so,' said Fliss, smiling. 'We've got my second cousin to find.'

When Fliss had left the room after dropping goodnight kisses on their cheeks, Laura looked across at the brown cardboard box on the table that her cousin had placed there when she'd arrived. There hadn't been time to look at the contents yet as Fliss had been a bit delayed in her journey getting here and Pete had already booked the table at the restaurant earlier in the day, so they'd had to leave the house almost right away to make their reservation on time.

Pete yawned and announced that he too was ready for bed. 'Are you finishing that drink?' he asked Laura, putting his empty glass down.

She nodded. 'I will in a minute. You go on up, love. I want to have a little peep in that box, just a quick look to see what there might be in there. I'll join you shortly.'

Pete smiled. 'Okay, love. Would you like me to stay with you, just in case there's anything in there that might upset you?'

Laura shook her head. 'I'll be fine. I doubt there'll be much of interest in there, but hopefully, there's some photos. There's no clue apart from the fact my name is written across the top of it and it looks like my dad's writing, but I can't be certain as it's a bit smudged. It'll probably be just a box that got forgotten about when they sold and emptied my family home. If Fliss and Harry hadn't cleared the loft at Aunty Lil's, I guess it would have stayed up there forever. She said it was tucked right under the eaves with a load of junk and covered in dust and cobwebs. At least she's wiped it down before bringing it over.' She laughed. 'I just hope no spiders have squeezed inside.'

'It's well taped up, so I doubt they will have,' Pete said and gave her a hug. 'I'll see you in a while.'

Laura studied the postcard-sized photograph of her dad. It had been black and white but was almost sepia now with age. He was young, fresh-faced and smart in his naval uniform, his dark hair neat under the white cap, smiling the wide smile she'd always loved, his big eyes twinkling at the camera. On the back he'd written, *For Mam and Dad, with love from your son Jack xxx*

Her heart filled with love for the man she'd adored and still missed so much. He would have enjoyed being a part of their noisy family and seeing his grandchildren and great-grandchildren growing up. He should have celebrated his ninety-second birthday this year; he didn't even make it to half that age, bless him. This photograph deserved to be in a lovely silver frame.

Maybe she could get a larger copy of the photo that would bring out the details more clearly. She'd look into getting that done and then choose a nice frame for it when she next went into the city. She placed the photograph carefully back in its envelope on the coffee table along with a few small photos of herself as a child, taken with Dad's Box Brownie camera, no doubt.

She opened another envelope and pulled out several more small photos. They were mainly of her paternal grandparents, who she'd never met, and Dad's brother and sister, who they'd seen from time to time as she was growing up. Dad used to take her to visit them if he wasn't working on a Sunday.

Her Uncle Tommy had passed away about ten years ago and shortly after that, her Aunty Jean had passed too. At least

Dad had been reunited with his family now they were all gone. The only other family Laura had ever known was her mother's sister Aunty Lil, and Uncle Ted and her two cousins, Fliss and Harry. Sadly, there had been no living grandparents on either side of the family.

There were only two small photographs taken of Laura with her mother in the envelope, she noted; the others were all with her dad. Well, that was fine, it was her dad she'd hoped to find. In both photos, her mother was pulling her usual pinch-lipped, unsmiling face and holding Laura awkwardly, like she hadn't a clue how to hold a small child.

There were none of her as a baby with her mother, just as with the few she had seen in an album that had come from a box from her mother's house, now residing in the loft here. She was an older baby and toddler in most of them and then a schoolgirl. Maybe her mum had suffered with post-natal depression? Looking at her mother in the two small photos, she could see that she really had been an unhappy woman, not unattractive in her own way, but not really the sort of woman she would have imagined that her fun-loving dad would choose to marry.

There was no resemblance to either Laura or her own daughters in her mother's features. Laura was like her dad in looks and colouring and her own eldest Rosie was like her and the youngest – Penny – more like Pete's family. With a sigh, she pushed the photos back into the envelope. She pulled out an old paper bag that held her dad's service papers, a photograph of his Second World War battleship, HMS *Warspite*, and also a couple of war medals on ribbons that she'd never seen before.

She felt emotional as she thought about the young boy, still in his teens, helping to fight a war and not knowing if he'd ever see his family again. As she held the medals in her hands, she felt so proud of her dad and the thousands of other young men like him, some of whom never came home. She placed the medals and the rest of the contents back in the envelope. Maybe she could get a small case or something to display his medals and the *Warspite* photo in. That would look nice alongside his photo in a smart frame; a little shrine on the sideboard where they could light a candle on his birthday and his anniversary.

As she made to place everything back in the box, she noticed the flaps inside the bottom of it were lifting up. She tried to flatten the cardboard down again but something seemed to be obstructing it. As she ran her hand alongside the edges of the flaps, she realised that they were creating a false bottom. There was a gap underneath, between the box bottom and the flaps, and something was wedged inside that gap.

Laura gasped as she lifted up both flaps on each side of the box to find a large bulky envelope that seemed to be full. There was nothing written on the envelope and it looked quite old and a bit crumpled, but it had obviously been hidden away purpose-fully for some reason. But by whom?

From what she'd seen so far, there was only her dad's hand-writing on the envelopes and the backs of a couple of the photos. There was nothing of her mother's in here, apart from those two photos with Laura so this must have been her dad's box, maybe some of the stuff he'd brought with him from home when he married her mother, as well as a few treasured photos of his family from many years ago. It had no doubt been shoved in the loft at home, forgotten about and then transferred to Aunty Lil's loft during the house clearance following her moth-er's death, while Laura was still resident at The Pines. Lil and Ted had obviously not got round to checking the contents; the tape on the box had been secure, with no signs of tampering.

Laura opened the envelope and pulled out a sheaf of papers. On top of the papers was an envelope with her name written on it, the ink faded now, so it must have been written many years before, and two small black-and-white photos of a pretty young woman holding a tiny baby wrapped in a shawl. On the back of each photograph was written *Katy and Laura*.

She frowned and opened the three-page letter that was inside the envelope. Laura took a deep breath as she saw her dad's handwriting and she started to read:

10 May 1953

My dearest Laura, today is your sixth birthday and I feel I need to write this letter to you. I've no idea if or when you will ever read it, but I need to write it anyway, just in case. It will be hidden away until my things are cleared and sorted when anything happens to me. I feel I have let you down, my darling girl, and I am so very sorry, but I have no idea how to make things right. I have to tell you that my wife Audrey is not your real mother. I married her when you were just over a year old.

Your real mother, Katy, was the love of my life and waited all through the war years for me to come home and marry her. Early on in her pregnancy with you, she was diagnosed with breast cancer. She chose not to start treatment until after she gave birth as she didn't want to harm you, but after you were born the cancer had spread and we couldn't do anything.

You were just six weeks old when Katy died in my arms. The photos in with this letter were taken a couple of weeks before she passed away. My sister, your Aunty Jean, took us in and while I worked, she looked after you. But she had her own family of four to bring up and I knew I had to find an alternative way of taking care of you.

I met Audrey, who worked at the Town Hall Registry Office, when I went to register your birth. She helped me as the registration was not as straightforward as normal with your mum being deceased. I'd left it a bit late to register you but I'd been so busy in those few weeks of looking after Katy and you, there hadn't been the time.

To cut a long story short, Audrey had been kind and helpful with getting a complicated declaration of parentage

*certificate sorted and she kept in touch with me and I asked
her out for a drink a few weeks later. We got quite friendly and
I eventually asked her to marry me as I thought she'd make a
good mother to you as well as a decent wife to me.*

*I'd told her my sister took care of you while I worked.
What I didn't realise was that she expected you to continue
living with my sister after we were married. I'm afraid I was a
bit naïve and when she told me she couldn't have children of
her own, I thought she'd be that thrilled to be bringing you up
with me. But I'm afraid I was very wrong. I bought us the nice
house we are living in now after inheriting a bit of money from
my parents and the house is in my name only and will go to
you when anything happens to me.*

*She's not put a penny towards it and gave up work right
away when we got married. I thought the house would be a
loving home for us all, but Audrey doesn't seem to know the
meaning of the word 'love'. Whatever age you are now, Laura,
you will no doubt have realised this fact and will be aware that
Audrey is very jealous of our father/daughter relationship and
also of my late wife, your dear mother.*

*She will not have Katy's name mentioned under our roof,
which is why I've never been able to tell you about her, even
though I am desperate to do that.*

*I have tried to get her to leave but she's having none of it
and she won't hear of divorce as she says it will shame her in
front of her family. She's threatened several times to do herself
in if I try and get a divorce. She admits she doesn't love either
of us but likes the status of marriage and having a nice home.*

*I don't love her; she's a cold-hearted woman and I found
that out when it was too late. I am worried that if anything
happens to me, she will not treat you right. I have made a
will, which is with my solicitor, and the details are in the big
envelope that you found this letter in. I have a heart problem;
the same as my mother had. I am taking medication for it and*

you have not been told this as you are too young to understand.

I hope I live to a ripe old age with all these tablets and get to see you happily married with children of your own. But that is a long way off; you are still a little girl as I'm writing this and I hope you don't get to see this letter for years yet. I have to make an apology to you for your birth certificate, which was redone by Audrey in the office she worked at shortly after our marriage. It's not your original one, which is in the big envelope. Your dear mother Katy's name is on the real one. She is buried at Southern Cemetery and details of the grave are also in the envelope in case you would like to go and visit.

I have to go in secret to take her flowers on her birthday and our anniversary but, if I am no longer around, there is no one else to do this. I hope you can find it and maybe will continue my tradition. I am so sorry if all of this confessing of mine is a huge shock for you, my dear daughter, but like I say, I'm trapped in this loveless marriage and I know I've trapped you too and denied you the love of a good stepmother. For that, I cannot forgive myself.

I hope one day that you can find it in your heart to forgive me once you learn the truth. Neither of us deserves Audrey in our lives, but walking away from her is impossible right now. I don't want her death on my conscience; that really would be hard to live with. I will make sure that you have the best childhood I can manage to give you for as long as I'm around and I know you will shine at school and build on a good future. With all my love forever, my dear girl, your loving daddy xxx

Laura wiped away the tears that had cascaded down her cheeks as she'd read and then reread her father's words. It was hard to take it all in, but a lot of what he'd written made complete sense when she thought of the way her life had been during her childhood and teens. If only she'd known all this in

1964, just a few short months after her father's death, life
would have been so very different. There would have been no
way her mother could have done what she did and packed her
away to The Pines.

Even if her mother had never found this letter, surely there
must have been evidence of her dad's will and the fact the
house had been left to Laura? Her dad's solicitor would surely
have tried to contact her at her Didsbury home and she was still
living there when he died. There was something not right about
all this. Okay, so the house had been sold *after* her mother's
death and the money put into trust and given to Laura when
she'd turned twenty-one. She and Pete had been able to buy
their first home and eventually this one they lived in now
without too much of a financial struggle.

But that house was hers and she should have been the one
to decide what happened to it. Ultimately, her mother had had
no legal rights to be there after her father died and it would have
given Laura the leverage she desperately needed when she was
locked away in The Pines. She could only assume that any
letters from the solicitor had been hidden away as soon as they'd
arrived and been dealt with by her mother and maybe Lil and
Ted, because of Laura's young age at the time as well as
Audrey's own selfish greed.

Laura gritted her teeth. She had to stop thinking of that
cruel and thoughtless woman as her mother from this moment
on. The cause of her death had always weighed heavily on
Laura's shoulders, because Audrey had said she had felt
ashamed of Laura's condition. She'd made Laura's dad unhappy
and caused him stress that probably contributed to complica-
tions with his heart condition. And, because of Audrey, she and
Pete had lost their precious son to strangers.

She stared at the tiny photos of herself and Katy, her birth
mother, and felt her heart breaking. This was such a lot to take
in and her head felt like it was spinning. She decided not to

wake Pete up now, as right at this moment she couldn't find the words to talk to him about it. It could all wait to be discussed in the morning – and also, she would see what Fliss had to say when she read the letter. Although it would seem that Fliss and Harry had both been kept in the dark about Aunty Audrey not owning the house, or Fliss would have had something to say about it before now, Laura was sure. And she was sure they didn't know about Katy, her real mum.

EIGHTEEN

BOLLINGTON, CHESHIRE

September 1964

On Wednesday afternoon Laura and Anna waited on chairs in the dining room that was doing double duty as a maternity clinic. In a screened-off area at the top end of the room, Barbara was having her monthly antenatal check-up. Anna fidgeted to get herself comfortable on the hard wooden seats that had been put out to form two rows for the waiting girls. Most of them had now gone back to their afternoon duties, each one sighing with relief as they finished being poked and prodded by the pair of nuns who were midwives, although Barbara often said they'd probably done no more training than a first-aid course.

Laura glanced at Anna, who she thought was looking paler than ever today, with dark circles beneath her blue eyes. They'd been in the laundry since eight thirty that morning and were both exhausted by lunchtime. Anna's ankles were swollen and she kept reaching to massage her back with both hands. Her baby bump was huge now, she'd doubled in size this week. Laura smoothed her dark-blue cotton smock top down over her bump and thanked her lucky stars that hers was quite small for now.

She was due in three months and knew that she could have hidden it well enough under tight girdles if she'd been given the chance to stay at home. She sighed; no point in going over that one again. She hoped that Pete had received her last letter via Lydia and Mary. If he had, he'd probably already written back to her by now, so hopefully, it would be any day soon that she got another letter from him. Barbara appeared from behind the screens and told Anna she was next. Anna got to her feet and waddled away across the room. Barbara dropped down onto the seat she'd vacated and sighed.

'How did you get on?' Laura asked her.

'Okay, I suppose. Blood pressure was fine and my weight is good. They think I've about three more weeks to go, judging from the measurements they took from the top of my bump to the bottom, which is about right from my dates. If I haven't had it by mid-October, they said they will give me an enema to start me off. Bloody hell,' she whispered, rolling her eyes, 'it's enough to put you off sex for life!'

Laura stifled a grin. 'Not very glamorous, is it? It's a far cry from the nights of passion that ended us up in here.'

Barbara nodded. 'You can say that again. And my bloody ex Phil gets off scot-free while I'm stuck in here, having his kid.' She smirked. 'It'll be just his luck if he gets his new girl in trouble. Well, I hope he does. She won't let go as easily as I did. Serve him right.'

Laura smiled. 'Well, with a bit of luck, you'll be out of here soon.'

'Let's hope so. I can't wait to get my life back and start again. I'm sorry, little one,' she said, patting her bump, 'I wish I could give you all that you deserve.'

* * *

Anna struggled to climb up on the couch to be examined. Typically, neither nun gave her a helping hand, keeping their backs to her and pretending to be busy at the table that held a variety of medical implements. Anna was short and the couch was a bit too high. She huffed and puffed and eventually managed to heave herself up before lying down flat on her back. As she let out a huge sigh of relief, one of the nuns turned to her and ordered, 'Lift up your smock and expose your abdomen please, Miss Brown.'

Anna did as she was asked and held her breath while the nun palpated her baby bump from top to bottom. She measured the area with a tape measure and listened with a stethoscope at strategic points. Frowning, she picked up a metal trumpet-shaped instrument that Anna knew was called a pinard and pressed it firmly on Anna's stomach, moving it from area to area.

She beckoned for the other nun to take over and handed her the stethoscope too. Anna wondered why she was frowning. She could feel her baby wriggling around, so she knew it was definitely still alive and kicking. She flinched as the first nun listened again with the pinard pressed a little too firmly near her bladder area and hoped to God she wouldn't disgrace herself. She should have popped to the lavvy before coming behind the screens.

The second nun nodded her head and said she would ask Sister Ursula to have a listen. She dashed away and Anna moved herself up the couch and leant up on her elbows. 'Is everything okay?' she asked the first nun.

'Yes, everything is fine,' she brusquely assured Anna. 'Sometimes we just need a second opinion. Please lie back down again.'

As Anna lay down again she heard Sister Ursula's voice coming closer and then she marched in, thrusting the screens away as she bustled through. The first nun pulled them closed as Sister Ursula picked up the pinard and repeated what the other nuns had done. She nodded her head, whispered something to the first nun and left the confined space as quickly as she had arrived.

The first nun checked Anna's blood pressure and took a quick look at her ankles, and then ordered her to sit up and pull her smock back down. 'It would appear that you are expecting twins, Miss Brown. There are two strong heartbeats and you are definitely much bigger than we would expect you to be at this stage of pregnancy. We will inform Sister Celia this afternoon and she will have a chat with you about your future care for the next few weeks. It's hard to say at this stage when the babies are actually due, but I would estimate that they will arrive in approximately eight weeks. We must ask you to keep this news to yourself for the time being. Now, if you would like to ask Miss Sims to come in as you leave. Thank you.'

Anna was hurriedly bundled out of the screened-off area before she had any chance at all to ask questions. She felt quite shell-shocked and it was all she could do to tell Laura it was her turn. Laura hurried off and Barbara jumped up to help Anna to sit down before she fell down.

'What is it?' Barbara asked. 'You're white as a sheet and you look like you're ready to pass out.'

Anna nodded. 'I feel like I am.' She looked around to make sure the nuns weren't watching her and whispered, 'I'm supposed to keep it quiet, but there are two in there.' She indicated her stomach with her thumb, her eyes filling with sudden tears.

'No!' Barbara gasped. 'Oh my God, Anna,' she mouthed. 'Wait until we're back in our room. We'll talk later.' She squeezed Anna's hand tightly.

* * *

'So how do you feel now?' Laura asked Anna as they sat on their beds after supper had finished and they'd been dismissed to their rooms for the rest of the night. Barbara was lying on her own bed across from them, trying to get comfortable on the thin mattress, where she groaned and declared that she could feel every spring digging into her weary body.

'Totally numb,' Anna replied, shaking her head. She'd been summoned to Sister Celia's office shortly after her check-up and had been told that she would be removed from any heavy laundry duties from tomorrow, but that she would instead need to help in the kitchen with the morning and after-noon tea breaks and evening meals and take on light daily dusting duties throughout the building. 'I can't believe it. It's like a nightmare. I can't lose two of them. I dare say it'll be a waste of time, but I'm going to write to my parents and beg them to get me out of here and let me go and live at Tony's mam and dad's house.'

'Good idea,' said Laura and Barbara together.

'I'll write to Tony's parents too but go via Lydia again for that letter. I can't see the nuns stopping me contacting my own parents, but they would stop me contacting Tony's, of course. They also said I had to keep quiet about the twins for now, not to tell anyone, but surely they must realise I have to talk to you two? After all, we share a room and you'd be bound to see my huge bump and say something to me about it.'

Laura nodded. 'Of course they must. They're crackers, the lot of 'em.' She patted her own baby bump and sighed. 'Well, *I've* only got one in here, thank goodness, and they said I'd be due mid-December. God knows what will happen between now and then. I still haven't heard from my aunt and uncle since my mother's death, so I've no idea what's happening with our family home and if they've put it up for sale or what. They haven't even bothered to write about Mum's death. At least the money from the sale will be mine eventually and will give me and Pete a great start in life when I can get out of this bloody dump.'

'And at least you know you've got a chance of a new life,' Anna said. 'I'm facing the great unknown with no idea what will happen. I'm terrified of giving birth to two babies here with no proper help at all. No doctors or nurses or anything.' Tears rolled down her cheeks and she wiped them away with the back of her hand. 'Oh God, I wish my Tony was still alive. I can't bear this pain any more.'

Laura put her arms round Anna, who sobbed heartbrokenly on her shoulder.

Two days before Barbara went into labour, she received another letter from Lydia and gave Anna and Laura their enclosed letters from Pete, and Tony's family. A couple of days ago she'd given them her home address and told them that if there were any problems getting letters to and from Lydia, they should do it via her.

'I know they don't like us to communicate with one another after the birth and before we go home,' Barbara began, 'but they have only stopped that one letter from Lydia and thankfully that was found in the bin by Olive. And the one I've just been handed now was also intercepted by Olive, she's just told me. But if I'm not here, Lydia won't be able to address them to me and Olive might not always be able to grab them first, so try my address and if my mother gets huffy, I'll send you my close friend's address and you can send the letters there and she'll pass them to me to forward on. I know it's all a bit of a faff, but it's better than nothing and at least it's contact with the outside world – and it's not for much longer now.'

'It is and we are very grateful,' Laura said as Anna rolled her eyes and wearily nodded her agreement. They each settled down on their individual beds to read their letters. Laura's eyes filled as she read Pete's heartfelt and sometimes angry words. He must be feeling so frustrated by the whole situation, she thought. If only she could talk to him on the phone. She just longed to hear his voice again.

My darling Laura,

I'm so sorry we are still unable to get you out of that godforsaken hole. I have been back and forward to your old home, trying to time it for when your aunt and uncle are there so I can have a go at them, but so far I haven't seen them. They have put the house up for sale already and it appears to have been emptied as I looked through the front room window and there's no furniture in there.

Surely this is your house now to sell? Have they been in touch with you yet to tell you what's happening? They told me the day I went round there when your mum had died that they're your legal guardians, but you're not a child so why on earth do you need them? You should be allowed to decide these things for yourself and could get a solicitor to help with all of the legal stuff.

I hope they don't steal your money. I doubt they will but it does bother me. I wish I could do more to help but I just don't have a clue what to do. Mick and I will ride past The Pines again the first week of November. I know it feels ages off, but you may not see this letter for a while so no point in saying we'll do it this week. We'll be there on the Friday morning about the same time as before. I really hope I get to see you again even if just for a moment. I can't stand this. It's doing my head in, Laura. I just don't know what to do for the best, love. I want to break in and kidnap you but I know I'll get arrested if I try anything like that and I'll be no use to you in prison.

I went to stand near your old house the day of your mother's funeral. I saw the time and date listed in the local paper's births, marriages and deaths page.

Your family didn't see me but your cousin Fliss did and she acknowledged me standing on the corner of the road. She said she'd write to you when I met her the day your mum died and she also said she wouldn't go to the funeral, but perhaps she didn't have a choice. I did wonder if maybe she could forward my letters on, but she's at uni and I don't have an address for her.

If you hear from her at all, ask her if that would be okay. Mary said she will write to you so at least it's some contact for you, but Fliss is family and the nuns might be fine with that. I hope everything is going well with the baby and it's doing alright and that you are keeping as well as you can and getting plenty of rest. I love you so much, my darling Laura, and I want to be with you, taking care of you, looking after you like I'm supposed to do. Write to me as soon as you can, I miss you so very much. All my love, always and forever, Pete xxx

Anna turned onto her side and tried to get comfortable as she read Tony's mam's letter. The news was pretty much as she'd expected; Dot and Frank had seen a solicitor but, as Anna was not their own flesh and blood, there was little he could do legally to help them. Anna was still under the control of her parent or guardian until she came of age, which was currently twenty-one. Dot asked her to keep in touch as often as she could and they promised they would continue to seek a solution if possible.

Anna sighed and folded the letter. She wondered what they would say when she told them there were two babies now. She was sure that Dot would be hammering on the door here once she got the news. Ah well, they'd all have to wait and see and keep hoping for a solution.

* * *

On Friday afternoon, as she was finishing off in the laundry room, Barbara experienced the first twinges of labour. She caught her breath and closed her eyes as the wave of pain passed through her. She carried on folding the towels and sheets, waiting for the next twinge and wondering if maybe it was one of the practice contractions that the girls had been told were called Braxton Hicks contractions. It just meant that the baby was getting ready but wasn't quite going to be born yet, and they'd been told that if they happened in the night, they were not to disturb any of the nuns until the pains were coming every two to three minutes apart. Barbara bit down on her lip and closed her eyes again as another surge of pain came.

Laura tapped her arm and frowned. 'Are you okay? You look a bit flushed.'

Barbara nodded. 'I think I've started. I've only had a couple of pains so there's no need to panic just yet, but I think this might be it.'

'Well, it's nearly brew time, five more minutes, so see how you are before we come back in here to finish off our shift. Anna should be in the dining room, helping Olive, so we can tell her then.'

As the pair walked into the dining room a few minutes later, Barbara holding on to Laura's arm, Anna waved them over to their usual table. Barbara perched gingerly on a chair and Laura went to get their mugs of tea from Olive.

'You okay?' Anna asked. 'You don't look very comfortable.'

'I'm not,' Barbara whispered, pushing a straying lock of dark-brown hair behind her ear. 'I'm getting pains. I'm going to time them when I've had my brew.'

'Oh, wow. This could be it, you're nearly free to go.'

'Yep. But I'll drag it out as long as I can before they cart me off up to the delivery room.' She stopped and half-smiled as Laura brought a tray of tea and cake over to the table. 'Thanks, Laura. Fingers crossed I can hold off until after suppertime and have an hour or two in our room so that I can get my case packed and ready to go. I'm a week or so early but I guess that doesn't matter when I'm almost full-term.' She lowered her voice. 'If you want to write any letters, get them done tonight when we go upstairs. I'll post them as soon as I get home.'

Laura and Anna nodded. 'Drink your tea now,' Laura said. 'Then we can get the last hour out of the way in the laundry. Are you sure you feel up to it? Let Sister Ursula know and then she may let you go to our room for the time being.'

'I will,' Barbara said, taking a sip of tea and grimacing slightly. 'Ooh, and there's another one. Don't think *these* are the practice ones.'

* * *

As Laura tried to sleep that night, she could hear Barbara's screams for help on the floor above them. She said a silent prayer that all would be okay for her friend and her baby. Why on earth the nuns couldn't give some pain relief she didn't know. It seemed cruel and barbaric to let the girls go through such pain. Each time, after the birth, there was sudden silence, as though they'd been sedated. During their pre-bedtime chats, all three of them had stated they dreaded the day labour would start, but at the same time, the sooner their babies were born, the sooner they'd be out of there. It was the unexplained silences at the end of labour that worried Laura most.

What the devil happened up there?

She and Anna had written their letters and they were now stashed safely away in Barbara's packed suitcase, hidden beneath her clothes. Laura had written to Fliss, as well as Pete. Fingers crossed, the letters wouldn't be found. Once Barbara's baby arrived, it would be kept wherever they kept the babies after their birth and then they would both vanish into thin air, as seemed to be the custom at The Pines. The baby to its adoptive family, Laura presumed, and Barbara back to her mother's house, without first being able to say goodbye to anyone. Why did the nuns do that? If everything here was supposed to be above board then why was the whole process so secretive? Some things just didn't add up at all. What did the nuns have to hide?

NINETEEN

BOLLINGTON, CHESHIRE

November 1964

All week prior to the day Pete had told her he was coming up to Bollington, Laura had racked her brains, wondering how the heck she could get out of The Pines. The only thing she could think of, and it was hardly a plan, was to try to get in the back of the gardeners' van while it was parked on the drive. It would have to be done before she gave birth, as afterwards the nuns would be sure to sedate her so she'd be capable of doing nothing, never mind escaping with a baby in her arms. It was worth a thought and she'd try to take her chance.

The first Friday of the month arrived and Laura felt like a cat on hot bricks as the clock on the laundry room wall ticked the minutes away even slower than usual. She was dying to get out into the garden for her mid-morning exercise stroll. Today was the day Pete had said in his letter that he and Mick would ride up and down Dumbah Lane in the hope that he would get to see her.

Sister Ursula, perched on a well-upholstered, comfortable chair in the corner of the room, was watching every move they all made with narrowed eyes and lips tightly pursed. Three girls came back inside and the nun nodded at Laura and another girl, sixteen-year-old Helen, who had arrived at The Pines last week and had taken Barbara's place in their shared room. Laura and Helen left the laundry room, pulling on their jackets as the weather had turned chilly in the last couple of weeks, and hurried outside. Laura led the way down the path at the side of the large house and out onto the front garden.

Anna was ahead of them, taking her morning stroll on the arm of Olive, who was helping to support her as she was now due to have her babies any day. Laura called in their direction and Anna turned and waved. She and Olive waited while they caught up. Fortunately, the gardeners were working on the large back gardens today, which meant the girls could walk around the front garden – usually they were told to keep to the back. Laura heard the sound of engines coming from the lane, but this time there were no loud voices singing her and Pete's favourite song.

'You hold on to Anna's other arm,' Laura instructed Helen. 'I won't be a minute.' She smiled at Anna, who raised an eyebrow and smiled back as Laura hurried off down towards the gate just as Pete and Mick were turning their scooters round in the road ready to ride the other way. She wondered just how many times they'd ridden past The Pines in the last hour. Pete lifted his arm and then kept himself out of sight behind the high brick wall and hedge. As she'd hurried past it, she'd taken a quick look at the van parked on the drive, but, just as she'd feared, there was a large padlock across a bar that kept the two back doors firmly together. She'd have to try and find another way.

Butterflies doing cartwheels in her stomach at the thoughts of being close to Pete again after so long, Laura stole a quick look back at the house, wondering if she was being observed. How much worse could her life get anyway? she thought. The tall metal double gates were chained up and padlocked as usual and would remain that way until the gardeners left the premises later, when a couple of the nuns would accompany them to the lane outside to make sure they all left and then re-lock the gates. No one visited The Pines without a prior appointment, so there was no way Laura could just slip out and jump on the back of Pete's scooter to be taken to freedom either. As he reached for her hand through the gaps in the gates and squeezed it tight, she clung on to him, feeling tears filling her eyes. It felt so good just to hold his hand.

He spoke quietly, his voice filled with emotion: 'How are you doing, my darling? It's so good to see you. Are you feeling okay?'

'Yes, I'm alright,' she replied, a sob catching in her throat. 'There's so much I want to tell you but we haven't got the time. I'm missing you so much. This is horrible, it's cruel.' She paused and took a deep breath, terrified a nun would come creeping down the garden at any moment. 'When I have the baby, I will let Fliss and Mary know as soon as I can and tell them which day I hope to be released. I know that my uncle will pick me up, so will you try and be here too and then I can come away with you? There might even be a chance that Olive could call Mary with a message, if she can.'

'Of course I'll be here. And it would be great if Olive could speak to Mary. I'll come each day that week on the off chance you get out early. We'll try and drive by again next Friday and each Friday until you're ready. Don't let them take our baby, please. I love you so much, Laura, please take care. Mick said he might be able to borrow his mate's car and then we can bring you and the baby home safely. Can't rescue you both on a scooter, can we?'

'I promise I will take care and I love you too but I really don't know how I'm going to get the baby out of here, Pete.' She sighed and looked over her shoulder. 'I doubt they'll just let me walk away with it, I'd better go now before I'm missed.'

'I know, but better short and sweet than not at all,' Pete said. 'I wish I could kiss you. This bloody gate is in the way. Please don't worry, we'll try and think of something. Bye, my darling girl.' He squeezed her hand tightly again and held it to his lips for a moment.

Laura hurried away up the path to join the others, who were waiting for her to go back inside. She felt her heart pounding in her chest and struggled to hold back the tears.

'You okay?' Anna asked, reaching to hold on to her arm.

'Better than I was, but I feel so very sad. I want to go home, but I don't even have anywhere to call home now.'

'You will have next month, even if it's just the room Pete's got for the two of you. Once you're together again, anywhere will feel like home. Just keep looking forward. Come on, let's get inside before they come out looking for us.'

* * *

In the bedroom after supper, Anna produced a letter from Barbara that Olive had given to her earlier. She quickly read through it and passed it over to Laura.

'She's given us her friend's address as she says her mum's being a pain in the arse and she is going to leave home as soon as she can,' Anna told Laura. 'Poor Barbara, it sounds like she's not having a very good time of it.' She lowered her voice; Helen, the new girl, was semi-dozing on her bed and she didn't want to scare her while she was just settling in. 'Olive told me something a bit worrying while we were making the tea for break this morning.'

Laura frowned. 'What? You mean something about Barbara?'

Anna nodded. 'She said Barbara's baby didn't cry at first but he did a few minutes later. Olive said she had heard Barbara screaming and crept up to the next floor to listen – she knew that all the nuns were up there so she wouldn't be seen creeping around – and then it all went quiet and she heard one of the nuns saying he's not breathing. But then she heard one of them say yes, he is, and she heard a faint baby's cry before she crept away.'

'Oh my God, that's scary. So it was a boy, which is more than we normally get to find out?'

'Yes, but Olive said she didn't hear anything from Barbara, so they must have given her some sedation to knock her out at the end. She said the baby vanished the next day and then Barbara left two days later. Olive seems to be certain that there is a secret foster home nearby where the babies go to be looked after until the adoptive family takes them once the arrangements are made. They're definitely not kept here because Olive has had a snoop around in the past when the nuns are all in bed and there are never any babies up there for any length of time.'

Laura raised her eyebrows. 'Really? Well, that sort of makes sense, because we never hear or see a bloomin' thing. They don't let the mothers have any contact with the baby and, let's face it, there are no nursery nurses here, just them five cold fish, and I can't see any of them wanting to touch a baby that they consider is a sin.'

'Huh.' Anna tutted. 'Ridiculous to think a tiny, innocent new life can contaminate you. What a brainwashed bunch of Bible-bashers they are! What was it Jesus was supposed to have said? "Suffer little children, to come unto me, for theirs is the kingdom of heaven." Obviously, a bit of biblical text the nuns choose to ignore.'

Laura sighed and nodded and read Barbara's short letter. There was no mention of her baby boy at all; maybe it was just too hard for her to think about him. She was cross about how her unfeeling mother was treating her really badly and said she couldn't stand it at home any more and was going to move into her friend's flat at the end of the month.

She was hoping to go back to work soon, but had needed to take another couple of weeks off due to an infection contracted in her womb from the lack of care she'd endured here. She'd written down the address of her new flat and they were to write to her there if they could manage it. Or send to Lydia, who had now got her new address anyway. And to add insult to injury, her waste-of-space ex, Phil, was getting married next month in the local church to his new fiancée.

'Poor Barbara, bet she feels like chucking rotten eggs at the pair of them,' Laura said. 'I know I would if I was her.'

Anna nodded. 'Me too, he's an absolute rotter. She's better off without him and she'll realise that when she meets a new boy. One day when she's feeling better, she'll start to pick up the pieces of her life again. I'm glad you got to see Pete today, Laura. That must have perked you up a bit.'

Laura sighed and her eyes filled with tears. 'Yes and no,' she said. 'All we could do was hold hands through the gaps in the gate railings. If only they'd left them unlocked for the gardeners to leave the place, I'd have been out of here and on the back of Pete's scooter faster than greased lightning. But I guess I was lucky to see him at all. He's said he's going to try and come again each Friday now until I've had the baby. With a bit of luck, Anna, you'll soon be gone and by then I won't be too far behind you.'

Anna smiled. 'Hopefully. Meantime I'm going to try and get to know Olive a bit better while I'm working with her. She's a mine of information – there's all sorts stored away in that head of hers. She's opening up a bit more each day and when she's sure no nuns are listening, she tells me more of what she's observed over the years.

'I tell you what as well, I don't think there's anything wrong with her mentally, like Barbara said there was.' She tapped her head. 'I think she's been so badly done to all her life, maybe firstly at her home and then treated unkindly here for years, she's just got no self-worth left. But she takes in more than you realise. One day it'll all come pouring out, just you wait and see.'

TWENTY

BOLLINGTON, CHESHIRE

December 1964

On a bitterly cold day in the first week of December, Laura stood with Helen to one side of the old marble fireplace in the lounge, while Sister Ursula bossily took over supervising the decorating of the large room and the spindly pine tree that had been brought to the home by the gardening team. Laura chewed her lip, wondering if it was really worth bothering.

The poor pine tree looked like a reject from nearby Macclesfield Forest, which it probably was. The gardener had announced as he'd carried the tree indoors in a large red, sand-filled pot that it was a gift from him and his team. It was better than nothing, she supposed, but the Christmas spirit was at an all-time low amongst the girls who were still in residence. Most of the expectant mothers Laura had got to know during her stay had already been delivered of their babies and had now left to go to their respective homes. Sadly, a couple of the girls had made it clear they'd rather stay at The Pines for the foreseeable future rather than go home to parents who had shown them so little love and understanding when they'd needed it most.

Laura felt so lost and alone right now and was worried about Anna, whose twin babies had not survived their recent birth, according to Olive, who'd sat on the top stairs for as long as she could while Anna was in labour so that she could report any news back to Laura. Six days ago, Anna had gone into labour early in the morning, but had been terrified of going to the delivery room and had been firmly told off by Sister Ursula when she'd finally plucked up the courage late afternoon to tell her that her pains were coming every few minutes. She'd then been unceremoniously bundled up the stairs to the delivery room, with little assistance from the uncaring nun.

Laura had lain awake most of the night listening to Anna's agonised screams, which had gone on for hours and had woken up the whole house. All five nuns had been in attendance but no one had called a doctor out, although it had seemed obvious to Laura that one was needed; even an ambulance and a trip to the maternity department of Macclesfield Hospital might have saved the babies that Olive told her she'd heard had been girls.

As soon as silence descended and Anna's cries had ceased, a tearful Olive had crept hurriedly downstairs and into Laura's room with the sad news. The following day, she told Laura that a hasty funeral had been conducted and no one but the nuns was allowed to attend. Anna vanished without trace two days later.

Laura frantically demanded to know where her friend was – she knew it was unlikely she'd have been allowed to go back to her parents, who seemed to have completely washed their hands of their daughter when she had written to tell them her news about the twins. And Tony's parents wouldn't have been allowed to collect her, so God alone knew where she was. Sister Celia had told her that it was not her business to know where Miss Brown was. There had been some activity with cars on the drive in the last day or so, but Laura had been unable to observe who was getting in and out of them.

She turned to Helen and shook her head. 'It's no use, I can't do this,' she announced in a loud voice that attracted the attention of the remaining girls and the two nuns in the room.

Sister Ursula stared at her and frowned. 'Can't do what exactly, Miss Sims?' she snapped. 'We are getting ready to celebrate the birth of our Lord.'

'Celebrate? Huh!' Laura waved her hands around to indicate the paltry decorations festooning the walls and the sad excuse for a Christmas tree. 'How could you go ahead with this? This false and pathetically ridiculous charade, after what's happened to Anna and her poor babies? It's so disrespectful; have any of you nuns got a heart? Well, you know what? You can stick it. I don't want any part of it.' She flounced out of the room and hurried upstairs as fast as she could go with her cumbersome baby bump, which was now bigger than ever.

She sank thankfully onto her bed and closed her eyes, fighting the urge to cry as she knew that any minute there would be a nun flinging open the door and demanding she come downstairs and resume her duties immediately. She stroked her bump and spoke softly to it. She'd been feeling really uncomfortable for most of the morning and wondered if she might be starting in labour.

'Please hurry up and come, baby. We can't stay here, we've got to get out of this crazy place before they harm the pair of us.' It surely couldn't be much longer now. Pete had kept his promise of riding to Bollington each Friday and was just waiting for her to let him know when she was ready to leave here. She had nothing to dress her baby in, not even a blanket to wrap around it.

She'd have to steal the sheet off her bed. Needs must and there was nothing else. What if the nuns gave her some drug or other that would render her unconscious right after she delivered and she was unable to hold onto the baby and scream the place down before they snatched it away? She had to stay awake

and alert before they took it to send to the foster home that
Olive assumed all the babies were sent to.

How the heck was she going to do this? No one else had
ever succeeded in taking their baby home with them, as far as
she knew from talking to the other girls she'd got friendly with.
What the hell was she supposed to do? She hoped she'd have
the strength to fight them off if they tried to stick a needle in her
with some form of knock-out drops in it. As she lay there, going
over and over things in her mind, the door flew open and Sister
Ursula strode in, closing the door behind her.

'Have you quite recovered from your childish temper
tantrum?' the nun asked, a sarcastic tone in her voice. 'You're
needed downstairs in the laundry to begin your shift.'

Laura sat up, wincing as a twinge went around her back.
'Ouch,' she said, grimacing. She took a deep breath and stared at
Sister Ursula.

'Don't give me ouch,' the nun said. 'You needn't think
you're getting away with pretending to be in labour, idling
around up here when there's laundry to be done. Now get up
this minute and move yourself, you lazy girl.' She grabbed Laura
by the arm and tried to drag her off the bed.

Using all of her strength, Laura pushed Sister Ursula backwards with both of her feet and slid off the bed, breaking the
nun's hold on her arm and sending her staggering into the
closed door. As Laura held onto the headboard and tried to
stand upright, another painful twinge gripped her. 'Oooh, my
God,' she gasped and sucked in a deep breath. Then, 'Get away
from me,' she yelled as Sister Ursula made to grab hold of her
again. 'Just leave me alone. I think my baby is coming and, if
you hurt me, my boyfriend will be after you.'

Sister Ursula laughed in her face. 'We'll see about that. Stay
there.' She pointed to the bed that Laura had just vacated. 'I
don't want you back downstairs, causing more trouble. I'll send
Olive up with a drink in a while. You know the drill – when

your pains are two to three minutes apart or your waters break, whichever comes first, you will be taken to the delivery room.' She stormed out of the bedroom, slamming the door behind her.

Laura drifted in and out of a light sleep for the next couple of hours in between pains that were not too bad to deal with just yet and not too frequent either. She knew they'd get stronger as the afternoon wore on if they weren't just Braxton Hicks contractions, which she didn't think they were as she was so close to her due date. Yesterday, she had received the long-awaited letter from Aunty Lil, for what it had been worth. One page and the accusing content had sickened her as she'd read the words:

Dear Laura,

This is just to bring you up to date with what's happening with your financial affairs following the very sad death of your dear mother, who took her own life as she couldn't live with the shame she felt you brought on our family.

We have laid her to rest in our local churchyard in Wilmslow with other members of our side of the family, as I know it wasn't her wish to be buried in Manchester alongside your father and his relations. We have sold the house and have stored the furniture and belongings in a warehouse so that you can collect them when you are home. We have some boxes here in the loft that we will keep until you can take them away. The money from the house sale is in a trust fund that you can access when you are twenty-one. I expect we shall hear from you when you are ready to come home. From Aunty Lillian and Uncle Ted

And that was it; cold and to the point. No 'how are you's' or 'good luck' – nothing, not even a kiss. Was this supposed to make her feel guilty? Well, it didn't. It made her feel more angry than anything else. She turned over on to her side as a light knock on the door heralded the arrival of Olive bearing a tray with a mug of tea, a cheese sandwich and a small slice of Victoria sponge cake. Laura shuffled up the bed onto her pillows and smiled as Olive bumped the door closed with her backside. She placed the tray on the bedside table and perched herself on the edge of the bed.

'How are you feeling?' she asked. 'Helen told me what happened earlier. You're a brave one for standing up to them, I'll give you that.' She smiled and patted Laura's hand.

'Not really, Olive. To be honest, I'm bloody terrified of the next few hours. I don't want my baby to die, or for it to go to strangers either, but I've got no choice other than to let them hopefully deliver it safely and then I'll have to see what happens after that.'

'It's all you can do,' Olive agreed. 'Fingers crossed the baby will be okay and so will you. I'll try and sneak up to see you later if the nuns are not on the prowl.'

'Will you do me a favour, if at all possible?' Laura screwed up her face as another pain washed over her. She took a couple of deep breaths and reached into her bedside table drawer for a pen and paper, then wrote down Mary's home phone number. 'Please will you call my friend Mary as soon as you can and ask her to tell Pete the baby is on its way and that I may be coming home very soon? He'll know what to do.'

Olive nodded and pushed the paper into her pocket. 'I might be able to do that tonight if they are all upstairs with you. At least most of them should be. If not, the others will be in bed and I can sneak into the office.' She looked down at her hands and sighed. 'I'm going to miss you when you go home, Laura. You're the last of the only group of girls that's been nice to me since I've been here.'

'Oh, my dear Olive, that's so awful to hear. I'm so sorry.

Young Helen will need a friend when I'm gone and there'll be others needing your support who will fill our shoes soon enough, no doubt. I do wish we could find out where they've sent Anna off to, though. I'm really worried about her.'

Olive chewed her lip and sighed. 'I think I know where they've sent her. I overheard them making the arrangements on the phone. It's the same place they sent me, I think. They told me it was a convalescent home for people with mental instability. It's over Liverpool way.'

'Really?' Laura gasped. 'Are you sure?'

'As sure as I can be,' Olive replied. 'It's your best bet anyway. I'll bring the address up in a while, I have to go and get it from my room. I'd better be off now or they'll be after me for wasting time but I'll be back as soon as I can and before they rush you off upstairs. Hide the address away though, don't want them finding it.'

Laura managed to get through the rest of the afternoon by doing the deep-breathing exercises she'd read about in a magazine. It helped her to cope with each contraction, but just as the supper-time bell rang out, she knew she couldn't hold on for much longer. The pains were coming every couple of minutes at least. If she didn't get help very soon this baby would be born on her bed and then there would be trouble. The nuns would be hard pushed to hide this delivery from the rest of the girls.

She was almost tempted not to call for help, but knew she could not put her baby at risk, and the nuns did seem to know what they were doing at least some of the time. She clutched her stomach as she slid off the bed and went to open the door. She called for help from the top of the stairs and two girls from the bedroom down the corridor came hurrying to see what was wrong. 'Can you please tell a nun I'm about to give birth?' she gasped. 'Well, tell them I'm not far off anyway.' One of the girls stayed with Laura while the other dashed away as fast as her baby bump would allow her to move.

Just when she felt all her strength ebbing away and didn't think she could stand any more of the horrendous pain, Laura made one more valiant effort to push and felt the immediate relief as her baby slithered out of her body. As she tried to prop herself up on her elbows to look at it, she was shoved roughly back down again, just as she caught a glimpse of dark-brown hair and heard a loud wail. 'It's a boy,' were the last words she was conscious of hearing before a black mask like her dentist used for tooth extractions was forced over her face and she had no choice but to breathe in whatever was coming out of the mask.

Hours later, Laura finally came round to find herself alone and in a different room to the one she'd delivered in. She sat up, bleary-eyed, and in the semi-darkness tried to get her bearings. A lamp on the nearby bedside table threw a gentle light over the unfamiliar room.

She heard a slight tapping at the door, then it opened and Olive popped her head round. 'Just checking in to see if you'd woken up yet,' she said. 'You've been out a long time. I did come up earlier but you were still sleeping. I've brought you some tea and toast.'

Laura moved up the bed a bit as Olive slipped an extra pillow behind her head. She felt a bit dizzy and light-headed but was glad to see Olive, who handed her a mug of tea and sat down on a small chair next to the bed. 'Thank you, Olive. What time is it?' She glanced around the room but could see no sign of a clock.   ·

'It's just after midnight,' Olive told her. 'Everyone is in bed except for me. I didn't want to fall asleep before you woke up.' She lowered her voice. 'I've let Mary know and she will tell Pete. I expect they will send you home the day after tomorrow. I told her that as well, so she said they will sort something out and that Pete would try and come over each day until he got you.'

'And where's my baby?'

'I'm so sorry, Laura, but I have no idea where he is, where they've taken him. I've searched around the office for a clue, an address or something. A man and woman in a car came earlier, I think they're from the foster family. Your baby is alive though – I heard a nun saying he had a good pair of lungs on him. So you had a healthy little boy.'

Laura nodded, tears running down her cheeks as she vaguely remembered hearing her baby crying and seeing his dark hair before that black mask was forced over her face. 'I know, I saw him very briefly. If we could only find out the address of the fosterers, we could go and get him back. They must be somewhere local, surely?'

Olive shrugged. 'I guess so, but God knows where. I'll try again when I clean the office tomorrow if none of the nuns are around.'

'Thank you. Don't get yourself into bother with them though. You have to live here. At least I'm on my way now.'

'You're very lucky, Laura. I'd better go now just in case anyone is snooping around, although I doubt it, as they sleep so soundly – if no one is in labour, of course.' She rooted in the pocket of her dress and handed Laura a piece of paper. 'This is the address where Anna was sent. Hide it as soon as you can and good luck finding her. I will bring your breakfast up in the morning and clothes and toiletries and your suitcase from your room.' With that, Olive slipped out of the room, leaving Laura to try to collect her scattered thoughts about what had happened over the last few hours. Her head still felt muggy and she knew she'd been drugged with something that had been used to stop her screaming for help, but God knew what. All she could think about was her poor little baby.

As daybreak arrived, a weak light peeking through the thin

curtains at the window, Laura gave up on trying to go back to sleep. Each time she closed her weary eyes, bad dreams tried to invade her mind, the nuns trying to snatch her baby from her as she fled barefoot down the garden with him in her arms towards Pete, who was waiting for them on the other side of the locked gates. Her body ached for her baby, to hold him and to feed him.

At eight o'clock, Olive arrived with scrambled egg on toast and another mug of hot tea. 'Try and eat this, you need to keep your strength up,' she told Laura. 'Sister Ursula said to tell you that someone would be up soon to help you into the bath and then you can get dressed. That might mean they're sending you home today, which is a bit too soon in my opinion. But you can rest and recover when you get home. Don't do too much though, or you'll end up bleeding heavily and then you'll need to see a doctor. I'll bring your case and other stuff up before they come to get you out of bed. Don't forget to hide that address I gave you as soon as you can.'

Laura nodded. 'It's under the pillow. I'll put it in my case when you bring it up.'

Olive smiled. 'I'd better go now and carry on with my chores. I'll see you shortly.'

By half past eleven, a tearful Laura was seated in the hallway of The Pines waiting for her Uncle Ted. She felt tired, sore and uncomfortable as she fidgeted on the hard wooden chair. She went back over the last hour since Sister Benedict had come up to the room, helped her to have a quick bath and told her what would happen next. As the birth had been straightforward, there was no need for Laura to stay any longer and the nuns felt it was best she went home that day. Her family had been informed and would be with them before midday. When she'd demanded to see her son, Sister Benedict had told her that his new family would be collecting him that afternoon and that he was no longer her baby.

She was told that she had willingly signed the adoption papers shortly after his birth, giving her full consent to his adoption. Laura felt heartbroken as she knew she had not signed anything – she'd been in no fit state to do so after they'd knocked her out with that gas mask and would never have given her consent anyway.

She had demanded to use a telephone and threatened to call the police, screaming that they were kidnappers and baby thieves. She supposed now that it was no wonder they wanted her out of the way as soon as possible before she caused any further problems for the nuns.

As she sat there deep in thought, her suitcase and handbag by her feet, Sister Celia came out of her office to tell her that her uncle was by the gate in his car waiting for her and she would accompany Laura down the path to let her out. Laura got to her feet and picked up her case, not even looking at the nun. She felt sick, but also consumed with rage and anger, and just hoped that Pete would be parked up somewhere nearby.

As she followed the nun down the garden path, Laura turned to look back at the house and hoped she would never again see this hateful place. She said a little prayer in her head for Anna's lost babies and made a silent promise to her own baby that she would find him again as soon as possible. These nuns could not be allowed to get away with this.

Sister Celia unlocked the gates and pulled one back slightly as Laura slipped through, to see her uncle's car parked just to the side. Without looking back at the nun, she walked round to the passenger door of the car. As she got inside and placed her case down by her feet, in the wing mirror she saw a flash of red and knew it was Pete's scooter. He must have been waiting on Dumbah Lane all morning and it was a freezing cold December day too. A feeling of relief washed over her as, when her uncle indicated and pulled slowly away down Dumbah Lane, he started to follow them.

* * *

Keeping his eye on the car carrying his Laura, Pete spotted an opportunity ahead to pull in front of the Jaguar and make it do an emergency stop without putting himself or Laura and her uncle in danger. He'd been told by Mary that it was unlikely she'd have the baby with her, which was probably as well because Mick had been unable to get his mate's car to help with the mission. Just to get Laura home safely to Mick's shared house was Pete's aim for today; they would hopefully be able to go back and claim their child very soon.

He signalled that he was pulling out to overtake the car and, as it stopped at the small crossroads, Pete swerved right in front of it, causing the driver to stamp on his brakes just as he'd been about to pull out onto the road. Pete jumped off his scooter as the passenger door flew open and Laura climbed out, clutching her suitcase. He ran round the car to pull her into his arms and held her tight while she sobbed against his chest as her uncle turned off the car engine and got out of the driver's side.

'Laura's coming home with me,' Pete told the man before he could say anything. 'She no longer needs you or her aunt. I'll be marrying her next year, it's all arranged.'

'I don't think so, young man,' Uncle Ted began. 'I'm her guardian and she's coming home with me.'

'I am not!' Laura yelled at him. 'After what you've all put me through, I don't want anything more to do with you. I'll be talking to a solicitor as well as the police once I get home with Pete. You sold my dad's house without my permission. I think you'll find that what you did is against the law.'

Uncle Ted's ruddy complexion paled as he stared at her. He turned to get back into his car. 'Your Aunty Lil will have something to say about this, young lady, after all we've done for you,' he threatened.

'All you've done for me,' Laura echoed. 'And what's that exactly? I've been locked up like a prisoner for months, my poor baby boy has been snatched away to God knows where with God knows who. And I don't give a damn about Aunty Lil after reading the letter she sent to me – or you for that matter. Neither of you will be seeing me again unless it's in court.'

Uncle Ted made to grab her arm but Pete stepped in-between them and Ted took a step backwards. 'I think Laura has made herself quite clear, don't you?' Pete said quietly. 'Now I suggest you get back in your car and go home.'

Laura looked at Pete and smiled as Uncle Ted got back in his car. 'That told him. Come on, Pete. Take me home, please, and then we can begin our new life and start looking for our boy.'

TWENTY-ONE

WEST DERBY, LIVERPOOL

June 2015

Pete shook his head as he finished reading Laura's dad's letter and handed it to her cousin Fliss to read. He looked across at Laura, who was seated at the dining table, going through the contents of her dad's box again for the umpteenth time now, making neat little piles of papers and photographs. She beckoned him over. He sat down next to her and took both of her hands in his. 'Are you okay?' he asked, squeezing her hands gently. 'I mean, that letter must have been one heck of a shock to read on your own. Why didn't you come and wake me up?'

'Yes, it was a shock and I needed to sit quietly and take it all in before I shared it.' She smiled reassuringly. 'I'm fine, honestly. I just feel closer than ever now to my dad, knowing that he and I were related and she wasn't. I just wish he'd been brave enough to tell me about Katy, my real mother, though. How dare that jealous bitch stop him doing that? And to deprive me of the right to go with him to put flowers on her grave, too.'

Pete squeezed her hand.

'All the years he's been gone and I didn't know anything about her or that there's no one else to take her flowers and keep her grave nice and tidy. Well, that's what I'm going to do first of all; I'll phone the Southern Cemetery in Manchester and get the grave location. Her death certificate is also in this box, so it may help them tell me where we can find it. We can go and visit and then pick up your mum from Wythenshawe and bring her back here with us while we're over there. Two birds with one stone, so to speak. It's such a shame that my dad wasn't buried along with Katy, where they both belong.'

Pete nodded. 'It is, but they might not be too far apart, hopefully.' He picked up one of the tiny photos of Katy holding Laura. 'We can probably get nice clear copies of these done and have them made bigger. Even on this you can see what a pretty girl your mum was. She's got a lovely smile and she must have been quite poorly when this was taken too, God bless her.'

He looked up as Fliss joined them at the table and smiled as she gave Laura a hug. 'I don't know what to say, Laura,' she began, chewing her lip. 'Other than what a bitter and nasty piece of work Aunty Audrey was. An incredibly selfish woman. And to think that my own parents were in cahoots with her over this sickens me to my stomach, it really does. They must have known the house was yours to inherit after Uncle Jack passed away and yet they took her side.'

'Thanks, Fliss,' said Laura shakily.

'I'm absolutely horrified by the way all three of them behaved towards you. The fact that my parents sold the house while you were incarcerated in that hellhole beggars belief. And then leaving you carrying the weight of her death on your shoulders when you had enough to deal with was bang out of order. I know they say don't speak ill of the dead, but bloody hell, all three of them were beyond wicked in this matter. I'm so sorry.'

Fliss paused and wiped her eyes. 'And I know now that this makes us no longer cousins as we're not blood-related any more, but I don't want to lose your friendship, Laura. You're the only family I've got besides my brother Harry and you and your girls and Pete mean the world to me. I love you all.' Fliss's lips trembled.

Laura flung her arms round Fliss and hugged her. 'You silly thing, we love you too and you'll always be my cousin, blood-related or not, and so will Harry.'

Pete smiled at them both. 'Extended families are the norm these days, aren't they? The more the merrier. One thing about this box's contents that's made me think is the mention in your dad's letter about birth certificates. He said something about your official birth certificate, but the one you have in our files upstairs shows Audrey as your mother and it's never been questioned when you've used it, like for our marriage and your passport etcetera. Because Audrey worked in the registry office in Manchester, she had all the tools to fake a certificate just by entering the details she was given by your dad and then adding her own as though she was your actual mother. Everything was done by hand back then and filed away. Makes you think, doesn't it?'

Fliss's eyes opened wide as she realised what he was possibly hinting at. 'So what you're saying is that maybe all the nuns at The Pines needed was a person they could trust at their local registry office who could provide the adoptive parents with a genuine-looking birth certificate, as no original one would ever need to be filed?'

'Yes,' said Pete. 'They probably slipped them a few quid for their time and effort and nothing more was ever said about it. The adoptive parents went off with a new baby and the necessary paperwork that would never be questioned. If only we could prove those nuns were doing all this for financial gain and not for the love of God or their so-called good works, providing babies they assumed no one wanted to families who genuinely couldn't have a child of their own. Those families would have no clue those babies were stolen. But why declare some were dead and others adopted? That's the bit I don't get.'

Fliss shrugged. 'I've no idea, but I have a feeling we're going to be getting answers to that one eventually. That'll be a good place for me to start.'

* * *

As Laura and Pete waved Fliss off just after lunchtime, the phone rang and Pete went back inside to answer it.

'It's Inspector Jackson,' he mouthed to Laura. She shut the front door and sat down on the bottom stair while Pete spoke into the receiver. 'Yes, just hang on a minute while I check with Laura.' He placed his hand over the mouthpiece. 'Can he and PC Miles bring Olive over on Friday afternoon this week, about two thirty?' he asked.

'Yes, of course.' Laura nodded. 'That will be great. Tell him I'll bake a cake like I promised to do.' She laughed as Pete related what she'd said and then stuck up a thumb. When he'd finished, she took the phone from him and called Anna to let her know to come over on Friday. She was also coming round on Thursday so that they could both have a lesson in how to run the Facebook group Laura's daughters had set up.

Rosie and Penny had told Laura they were going to launch the group to go live and make Laura and Anna admins on Thursday, whatever that meant; but Laura was pretty sure she and Anna would soon pick up what to do. She couldn't wait. She hoped the friends they'd got to know well, like Barbara and Lydia, would get in touch via the group eventually.

If their birth certificate theory was true, then it was not going to be an easy task to trace the adoptees, but they had to give it a try. As she went to join Pete in the lounge, something Anna had just mentioned stayed in her thoughts. If none of the remains found in that garden were human, then there was every chance that Olive's child had also been born alive and not dead as she'd always been led to believe. That would be wonderful, because, as far as Laura knew, Olive Greaves didn't have a living soul in the world who belonged to her.

'Right, are you ready, Mum, Aunty Anna?' Rosie said as she positioned two laptop screens in front of her mother and Anna. 'I'll open up the Facebook site and pull up the page for you to look at. Then between us, we'll work out what to say on the pinned post that will attract people to read what the group's all about.'

Laura and Anna nodded and stared at the screens as Rosie pointed out various aspects of the group's site. At the top of the page was positioned a large picture of The Pines that they'd used as a header. The group title heading read *A group for Mothers and Adopted Children of The Pines, Bollington, Cheshire.* It was marked 'private', so only members could see what anyone else had written, to keep the privacy of the members, but it was also possible for anyone to find the group in a search.

'That's the best of both worlds,' Rosie said to her mother. 'Now we'll make you and Anna admins and when anyone wants to join, you will see a notification and then you approve them. We will put a couple of questions in there for them to answer and if you're happy that they are genuine then you just approve them. Are you following me so far, Mum?'

Laura chewed her lip and nodded. 'I think so, love.'

Penny smiled and said, 'Don't look so worried, Mum. Rosie and I are also admins, so each day we'll take a look and make sure it's all running in the right way. We won't just abandon you. Right, let's all add ourselves as members to get it off to a fine start. Then we can each make a post. Mum, you will be saying that you're looking for your son and we'll say we're looking for our brother and Anna can say she's looking for her twin daughters. That gets us off to a flying start, don't you think?'

'Yes,' said Laura, feeling excited and a little overwhelmed.

'After your visit with Olive tomorrow, I'll call my pal who works for the newspapers – he has contacts with the *Manchester Evening News* group, so we can get a bit of promotion in their paper too, and also, he may be able to get us a scoop on *Granada Reports* as that would really help. Seeing as both the paper and telly has already covered this and it's a real human interest story, I think they'll run something.'

TWENTY-TWO

DIDSBURY, MANCHESTER

February 1965

Laura picked up the post from the doormat and checked through the pile of envelopes to see if there was anything for her and Pete, and smiled as she saw there was a letter for each of them. She put the rest of the envelopes onto the hall table for the other tenants to look through when they came home from college or work. She took her and Pete's letters into the large and pleasant front room they called home for the time being.

A small sofa was pushed into the bay window at the street end with a coffee table in front and a TV stood on a unit in one of the alcoves. Their bedroom furniture was hidden behind a screened-off area at the back of the room. They shared the kitchen and two bathrooms with their neighbours. Laura didn't mind; anything was better than The Pines and most of the day everyone else was out and she had the place to herself.

She strolled out to the kitchen and made a mug of coffee before curling up on the sofa with her little black cat, Sooty, who had been returned to her by Fliss. Laura was so glad to be reunited with him and he seemed happy to be back with her too.

She picked up her letter and smiled as she recognised Anna's handwriting. They had managed to track her friend down from the address given to Laura by Olive. They had driven over to Liverpool two weeks ago with Mick in his friend's car, borrowed for the Sunday afternoon. Anna had been allowed to accompany them on a stroll around the gardens, but she wasn't allowed off the premises at that point.

Strathclyde Convalescent Home was a large house off Queen's Drive in Wavertree, and only a stone's throw from where Anna's late boyfriend Tony's parents lived. Anna had written to them as soon as she arrived at the home and they had been to visit her and told her she would always have a home with them, should she need it. Laura had written to her as soon as she could after arriving at Mick's shared house. Anna had written back immediately.

They'd arranged the first visit and during that visit, Laura could see, although Anna was still understandably very emotional when she talked about losing her babies, there was no sign of mental health issues about her at all. She was in complete control of herself, a far cry from what the nuns had told the Strathclyde staff when she'd been admitted. She was grieving, which was no surprise after losing her boyfriend and her daughters and being abandoned by her snobby parents, who had made it clear they were willing to pay for her to stay in Strathclyde for a very long time.

Laura took Anna's letter from the envelope and smiled as she read her friend's words while she sipped her coffee. Sooty stretched out his long silky legs and purred loudly. Anna wanted to know if they could go over to see her again this weekend. Hopefully, Mick would be able to borrow a car again, Laura thought, but if not, she and Pete could ride over on his scooter – as long as it didn't snow again. She'd need to have a look in the local paper to see if the long-range weather forecast gave details for Saturday and Sunday.

The snow had been falling intermittently for the last couple of months, ever since Christmas, but it was clear today and most of it had melted away. She popped Anna's letter back in the envelope and got up off the sofa, much to Sooty's disapproval. 'Don't be grumpy,' she scolded gently, stroking the top of his head. 'Come on, let's get you some stinky sardines for your breakfast and then I'm jumping in the bath while I've got the house to myself.'

As Laura soaked in the bubbles her thoughts went back over the last few weeks since Pete had come to collect her from The Pines. The first thing they'd done was consult the solicitor who Laura's dad had always used. She knew the address on Market Street in the city centre as she'd been to the offices with her dad when he'd been doing what he'd called *seeing to family business* after his sister passed away.

Laura and Pete made an appointment and went to see Frederick Symonds in the second week of January. Laura had consulted the notes she'd made prior to the visit, which included her dad's verbal declaration that she would inherit the house when anything happened to him and her mother. Now Mr Symonds shuffled through a mountain of paperwork that sat on his desk and nodded thoughtfully over a piece of paper that he informed her was her father's last will and testament, naming her as the recipient of his estate.

The company had written to Laura after her father died, but, as she had failed to respond, no further action had been taken. Laura shook her head, feeling shocked by this news. She had never seen any correspondence. When she went on to tell him that her aunt and uncle had sold the house after her mother's death, his eyebrows shot up his prominent forehead. 'The house was not theirs to sell,' he said. 'Without your permission, they should not have taken it upon themselves to do that.'

'Well, they did and they informed me the money is in a trust fund until I'm twenty-one,' Laura told him. 'But we need it now. We are hoping to get married early next summer and that money would buy us our first home.' She looked at Pete, who nodded. 'With both my parents gone, we don't need their permission and we have Pete's parents' blessing. Anyhow, we intend to marry over the border in Scotland.'

Pete nodded his agreement again. 'Tell him what your family did to you and why we need his help,' he urged her.

Laura took a deep breath and told Mr Symonds what had happened to her in the last few months. 'Can you help us to get our baby back? Please. It's not just the money we need, we want our child too.' Tears ran down her cheeks and Pete reached for her hand.

'And you say these nuns told you that you had given your permission and signed to say the baby was to be adopted?'

'Yes.' Laura nodded. 'But I didn't. I never wanted to give him away, neither of us did. They drugged me with something, I have no idea what, but they slapped a black mask over my face and that's the last thing I recall that day until I woke up much later and our baby had already been taken away by then. He was definitely stolen. Is there anything at all you can do to help us?'

Mr Symonds looked at her over the top of his wire-framed glasses. 'I'll do my best, my dear. I will write to this home and demand to know what happened. Meanwhile, I can try and get your money for you by overthrowing the trust fund ruling. We can use your father's will as proof that you are entitled to that money immediately. At least that will give you a good start for your married life. And then I will try my best to reunite you with your son. It's not easy to find a child who's been adopted unless we have some paperwork in front of us, but I will ask the nuns to provide anything they may have.'

'Thank you.' Laura got to her feet and shook the solicitor's hand across his desk and Pete did likewise. They left the office feeling more hopeful than when they went in.

Outside on the street, Pete pulled her close. 'All we can do is wait, babe. At least we've set the ball rolling.'

Laura nodded. 'Maybe next month I'll go back to college and finish my art course. It will help keep my mind occupied and make it easier for me to get a job for when we are married; we'll need the money for our new home. I feel like I've had a long enough rest now. I'm fully recovered from Paul's birth, so I should get my life back on track. And it will be nice to see Mary regularly again as well.'

Pete smiled. 'If you're sure, I'll support you all the way, you know that. I love the way we always call our baby Paul rather than just "he" or "baby". He feels more real with a name.'

'He does,' Laura agreed. 'Shall we go and get some lunch? May as well make a day of it seeing as you're not working today.'

'Why not?' Pete said. 'I'm starving, but you choose.'

Laura rolled her eyes and grinned, reading his mind. 'Burger King it is then. Lead the way.'

That night, Laura wrote back to Anna and told her that they would see her on Saturday afternoon, all being well, car- and weather-wise. She planned to take her a bag of nice toiletries to cheer her up, so a visit to Boots tomorrow was a must. Mick knocked on their door and asked if they wanted a brew as he'd just put the kettle on in the communal kitchen.

'Yes please, but don't forget to use the tea strainer,' Pete called after him. 'Laura can't stand floating tea leaves.'

'I know.' Mick dashed to the kitchen and brought back a

box, waving it at Laura. 'Tea bags,' he announced, grinning. 'We're moving up in the world. Got 'em especially for you.'

'Oh wow, now there's posh,' Laura said, laughing. 'Thank you so much. For that, you can share our chocolate biscuits with your brew.'

She put some biscuits out on a fancy plate and Mick carried in a tray with three steaming mugs of tea, which he placed on the coffee table.

'So, we're off to see Anna this weekend then?' Mick asked as he sat down on the carpet and leant back against the chimney breast. Laura chucked him a cushion to put behind his back to make it more comfortable. 'Be nice to see her again. She's a lovely girl who deserves better than she's had thrown at her in life so far.'

'She does.' Laura nodded her agreement. 'Be better for her when she can get out of Strathclyde. She shouldn't be in there at all. She's not mentally unstable, she's just a girl who's had nothing but shit thrown at her for the last couple of years.'

'Those bloody nuns have a lot to answer for,' Pete said, lighting a cigarette and puffing a cloud of smoke in the air above his head. 'I wonder just how many poor girls have had their lives destroyed by them. At least I got Laura back in one piece – apart from losing our baby to them, of course – but from what she's told me, some of the girls are leaving there complete emotional wrecks. That place needs shutting down. Hopefully, we should be hearing from Laura's solicitor soon about our Paul and if we can get him back.'

Laura nodded. 'And if we can get the house sale money too, then we can start looking at buying a home of our own this year for us and Paul.'

'That'd be great for you all,' Mick said. 'It's a good start in life to build on.'

. . .

Anna was waiting in the garden as they pulled up at Strathclyde on Saturday just after lunchtime. She looked cold, Laura thought, wondering why she had been waiting outside. She was wrapped up well, though, in a warm jacket and scarf, with a knitted bobble hat pulled over her thick auburn hair that was flowing halfway down her back. There was an air of excitement about her and her blue eyes were sparkling, in spite of the cold day and her little red nose. She waved them over before they got out of the car and went to the passenger door. Pete wound down the window and smiled at her.

'You okay, Anna?' he asked.

She nodded and spoke softly. 'Can you drive round to the back gate and wait for me, please. I'll meet you there in a couple of minutes.'

'Sure,' Mick answered and pulled away to drive round the block. He pulled up at a large green gate as Anna squeezed herself through a gap in the dense hedgerow next to the gate, dragging a suitcase along with her. Laura, sitting in the back behind Pete, leant across and flung open the door next to her and Anna climbed into the back passenger seat beside her and pulled the case in with her. She looked over her shoulder and sank down to the floor out of sight.

'Just drive away, quickly,' she ordered Mick. 'We can stop and put my case in the boot a few miles down the road.'

As Mick put his foot down and pulled away, Laura turned to Anna, who was still squatting almost on the floor. Her questions tumbled over one another. 'What are you doing? What's going on? Why the case, and why all the secrecy?'

'I'm running away,' Anna confirmed, half-smiling. 'I got up this morning and decided I'd just about had enough of being controlled by other people who think they know what's best for me. I want some normality back in my life. So, I'm taking charge and making it happen otherwise I'll be stuck in there forever at this rate. Will you take me back to Manchester with you, please?'

'Yes, of course,' said Laura.

'Thanks. I'll come back to Liverpool and Tony's mam's place after a while when the dust settles. I'll call her later to let her know where I am, just in case she plans on visiting me tomorrow. They won't miss me back at the home, because, once they inform my parents I've gone and they stop paying the fees, they'll all just wash their hands of me. I'm not registered with any authority and I wasn't admitted in there under the NHS, like most patients are. It was just a private set-up to keep me away from home for as long as possible.'

Laura grinned and shook her head as Pete turned to look at the pair. 'Well done, Anna. I'm sure we can squeeze a small one in at the house. What do you say, Mick?'

'We definitely can,' Mick agreed. 'There's a room just come spare next to mine. I'd love to have you as a close neighbour, Anna.'

Laura beamed at her friend as she blushed.

A couple of miles down the road from Strathclyde, Mick stopped the car. 'You're one crazy madam, you know that,' Laura said. 'But I mean crazy in a good way. Right, you can come up off the floor now and Pete will put your case away to make a bit more room for us back here before we begin the journey home.'

'Home,' Anna said, smiling, as Pete reached in for her case. 'You have no idea how good that word sounds.'

June 2015

Laura, Pete, Anna and Mick waited patiently in the lounge for Inspector Jackson and PC Miles to arrive with Olive. Laura's daughters had visited the previous day with the news that, depending on how today's meeting went, Laura and Anna were possibly going to appear on *Granada Reports* on Friday with an appeal and to promote the Facebook group in the hopes of bringing people forward who might be able to throw some light on the investigation or might know someone who could.

So far there had been several new members added to the group. No one they knew personally yet, but all of them, a mixture of male and female, seemed to have a connection with The Pines. Laura had studied each male profile picture in the hopes of recognising something in the features that might look familiar, but there was no one who she felt could have been Paul.

All the younger people in the group were hoping to connect with a family member who might be able to throw some light on their beginnings. As was expected, no one so far had anything other than a normal birth certificate with the names of the parents they believed to be their birth parents. But most seemed to have one thing in common; for one reason or another, they believed they had been adopted at birth from The Pines.

Pete went over to stand by the window to keep an eye out for the car that would be bringing their visitors. At exactly two thirty, a sleek black Audi saloon pulled up at the end of their drive. 'They're here,' he announced and threw open the door to greet Inspector Jackson and a small, plump lady with neat grey hair whom he presumed to be Olive, on the arm of PC Miles. 'Come on in,' Pete welcomed them. He led the way into the lounge and Laura and Anna jumped to their feet and held open their arms as Olive smiled shyly and moved towards them. She was enfolded and hugged and kisses were dropped on her cheeks.

'Olive, it's so good to see you,' Laura said. 'After all this time. It's been so long.'

Olive wiped away tears from her cheeks and Anna handed her a box of tissues from the coffee table. 'Come and sit down with me and Laura,' she suggested as Olive removed her coat and handed it to Pete, who took it to the hallstand to hang up. 'I can't believe you're here. We always thought about you, didn't we, Laura? We did actually write to you a couple of times, but we didn't hear back so we assumed you'd left your job, or just didn't want to keep in touch.'

Olive shook her head. 'I was never given any letters from you,' she said quietly. 'They stopped me from doing the post after you two left. One of the nuns got suspicious and I think they threw away more letters than they gave out from then on. They never liked me being friendly with any of the girls, as you know, and after you two left, I didn't bother with anyone else again. I just kept meself to meself until they closed the place down and told me to leave.'

'Oh, Olive, how have you managed since that happened? I mean, I know they were awful to you, but it was the only home you really knew for years,' Laura said, with visions of poor Olive living in a cardboard box in a shop doorway. Although she had to admit that she looked neat and clean and well cared for today.

'While you girls catch up,' Pete said, 'I'll make us all a brew and slice that cake you made, Laura. Come and give me a hand, Mick, and then Inspector Jackson and PC Miles can have the chairs to relax on; we'll park ourselves on the floor.'

'Bring some dining chairs through for you two,' Laura suggested. 'No need to sit on the floor, we're not living in that student house any more.' She sat down on the sofa next to Olive, who was now sandwiched between her and Anna. She took Olive's hand and smiled at Inspector Jackson. 'You have no idea how good it is to see Olive again,' she told him. 'Thank you so much for doing this.'

'Believe you me, it's our pleasure and to see Olive looking so happy is worth its weight in gold. Told you we'd look after you, my dear, didn't I?'

'You did,' Olive agreed. 'I've been so worried about coming forward,' she confessed to Laura and Anna. 'But after seeing the appeal on the telly, I knew I had to do it while I'm still here. After everything that went on there and all that I saw and heard, I knew I couldn't let it go. I would never have forgiven myself.'

She told Laura and Anna what had happened to her after leaving The Pines. A local doctor had become involved in her care just before she left the home for good and had reported to social services that he had a vulnerable adult female patient who needed urgent accommodation. Olive was found a smart one-bedroomed flat in Macclesfield in a small block for people of mixed ages, most with special needs or health problems.

She had her own space and independence and from day one had thrown herself into helping the on-site manager to run the place. She'd soon got much better and told them how much she loved her job, felt valued for what she did and that she actually got paid for the work as well as getting her flat rent-free because the council paid it for her.

'I've never felt so needed or well off in my life,' she finished. 'I can buy myself new clothes when I need them and nice soap and stuff.' She paused for breath. After years of saying very little to anyone, it was as if someone had found Olive's 'on' switch. 'And I go to the local church, which isn't Catholic,' she continued, 'and I was persuaded to speak to the vicar, who told me that what the nuns had threatened me with for years, that I'd be struck down dead by God if I told anyone tales about The Pines, simply wasn't true. They were nasty swines to us all, weren't they, girls?'

'They were indeed,' Laura agreed. 'It's probably as well none of them are still alive now, as I have a feeling they would be in a heck of a lot of trouble with what's come out since the first remains were found.'

'Aye well, perhaps *they* got struck down for all the nasty things they did by pretending to be good and kind. The real God and good nuns wouldn't do half of what those five were guilty of, according to my vicar. He said God only wants good things to happen to people. I mean, look at you two now – you're so happy, and I'm really glad about that after what you both went through.'

Olive had her handbag on the floor by her feet and she bent to open it and pulled out a tattered notebook. She placed it on her knee as Pete came in with a tray of mugs, followed by Mick with a large, sliced chocolate cake and a stack of small plates. 'Them's me notes,' she told Laura and Anna. 'What I wrote down over the years and hid underneath the mattress on me bed. It's all in there, I tell you. All these years I've had to keep quiet in case I got struck down dead for telling the truth but I'm ready to share it all now.'

Laura held her breath as Olive continued. 'They were in it to make money, you know. That's what it was all about. Them rich Americans coming over here to adopt babies for thousands of pounds and some of our poor girls being told their babies were dead. There might have been one or two that did die as they weren't looked after properly when they were being born, but not as many as they made out. And most of the girls didn't want to give the babies up either but they were told they'd signed them away. All lies.'

Laura swallowed hard. 'Like I was told I'd signed my baby away.' Olive nodded. 'Yes, exactly like that.' She looked at Inspector Jackson, whose eyes had lit up at the sight of her notebook. 'I'll go through this with you, every page, as you might not be able to make head nor tail of my writing, but it's all here and will help you to understand what went on at The Pines.'

Inspector Jackson smiled at PC Miles. He was told to help himself to cake by Pete and his smile grew wider. 'I told you she wouldn't stop once she started,' he whispered, nodding towards Olive. 'She just needed the confidence to realise she'll be safe, that no one will harm her. That notebook will be a mine of information.'

'I think you're right there,' PC Miles agreed with a smile back. 'I can't wait to see what she's written. Best idea of all, bringing Olive here today.'

Inspector Jackson's brown eyes twinkled. 'I think we're going to have a very informative and productive afternoon and beyond. And that cake looks amazing.'

. . .

By the time the two police personnel and Olive had left, Laura and Anna had promised to stay in touch with Olive and speak to her regularly on her mobile phone. They had put both their numbers in for her, so that she would know who was calling, as she was still a little wary about answering the phone: 'In case it was someone after her blood,' as she put it. Mick and Pete decided they were hungry and went out to get fish and chips for tea.

Laura set the table in the dining room and while they waited, she and Anna fired up Laura's laptop to see if there were any new members to add to the Facebook group. PC Miles had asked if she could join the group on a purely observational level, so that she could keep a regular check on anything that struck her as needing further investigation.

Inspector Jackson had given them permission to speak on TV this week if they could get a slot. As far as he was concerned, the more exposure the group got, the better. Not everyone had use of a computer, but most people watched the TV at some point each day. A dedicated phone number was to be given out, manned by the police.

Laura thought back through everything Olive had told them, her mind still whirring. The adoption racket that had been masterminded by the nuns at The Pines had been purely for their own financial gain. But they were unlikely to find proof, as Olive had recorded in her notebook after seeing the nuns burning all the so-called official papers from the office in metal bins, just before she left The Pines in the late sixties. When she had taken a quick look in the office the following day, the shelves had been emptied of all the box files where the papers had been stored.

It seemed to add weight to the theory that, if things had been legal and above board, when The Pines finally closed down the paperwork would all have been passed to the authorities. Social services had done their own initial investigation after the rumours of numerous child deaths had been reported by people in the village and had eventually demanded that the home be closed down.

Olive's notes also stated that if a child had been legally adopted with the agreement of the mother, the nuns would charge a fee for that child and the prospective parents were usually what Olive called 'proper toffs with plenty of money'. They would be issued with a birth certificate and the child, once the agreed fees were paid in full. If a child had been declared dead to the mother at birth, and therefore untraceable, the nuns would charge twice the fee to the adoptive family.

'So when you think about it, they must have been over the moon when they told me I was expecting twins,' Anna said. 'Two for the price of one and then lying about them being dead doubled the price; they must have been rubbing their greedy hands together. They made a fortune out of me – and ruined my chances of ever having more children by the way they delivered them, ripping them from my body and then leaving me in that dreadful state. No wonder I was depressed. I could have died and they didn't give a shit. Hateful witches! I hope they're all burning in hell.'

'Me too,' Laura said. 'It's no more than they deserve. Like the inspector said, it's illegal trafficking, but because there's no one left that's accountable, they can't charge a single soul.' She stared at the screen for a moment and then said, 'Ah, there's PC Miles, she's asked to join us, and there's five others as well – flippin' heck, we're growing in numbers. There are quite a few more members than there were this morning when I last looked. Maybe our Rosie and Penny have approved them for us.'

'At this rate we should find almost every baby that ever got sold from The Pines,' Anna said hopefully. 'Look, some have even put pictures of their birth certificates on in their posts.'

'Blimey, yes,' Laura agreed. 'We may well be lucky. Ah, the men are back with our fish and chips. I'm starving. Let's get stuck in and then we'll have another look at the group later to see if anything has been added to it.'

Laura and Anna sat nervously in a small waiting area with Laura's daughters for company. They were due to be interviewed by a TV presenter for tonight's *Granada Reports* programme. A young woman beckoned them forward and they followed her down a narrow corridor and into the studio beyond. The presenter welcomed them and, as the programme went live on air, he introduced himself and his guests, told the viewers why they were here and encouraged them to speak about their Facebook group.

Laura spoke first and then Anna, losing her initial shyness, joined in. They explained why they had started the group and that they hoped that by appearing on TV tonight, they would encourage people who may feel, or know, they'd been adopted and wanted to trace their birth families. Although they might be having problems because there was no official paper trail to support them, they should come forward as they could be a child who had been illegally sold many years before.

DNA testing could be arranged to help the process and, if copies of the birth certificate that was issued at the adoption could be scanned and posted to the group or emailed to the address on the group page, it would also help with the tracing process. Laura assured viewers that everything would be kept confidential within the confines of the private group and with the police officers that were assisting with everything. She also told viewers that she and Anna were searching for their son and daughters and were hoping that this plea would help them.

As they came off air, Laura and Anna were invited for refreshments by the green room staff, along with Laura's daughters.

'Well done, Mum and Aunty Anna,' Rosie said, giving them

both a hug. They sat down at a small circular table. Penny had collected a tray of coffees and biscuits. 'That was great, you did well. It can't have been easy for you both but let's hope something good comes from this now. You really do deserve it. I just hope and pray that we find our brother after all this time.'

Laura's eyes filled and tears spilled down her cheeks. She took the tissue her daughter held out to her. 'Oh, so do I, Rosie, so do I. That would be a dream come true for me and your dad.'

TWENTY-FOUR

DIDSBURY, MANCHESTER

April 1965

Anna woke to a gentle knocking on her bedroom door. She turned and glanced at her alarm clock on the bedside table; it was just before eight o'clock. 'Come in,' she called, knowing it would be Mick with her early morning brew. He'd taken to bringing her a cuppa each day since she'd moved into the shared house. It was a nice feeling having someone else caring about her as well as Laura and Pete. She sat up as the door opened and Mick carried two mugs of tea through. 'Morning, Mick,' she said, and smiled at him, 'and thank you.'

'It's my pleasure,' he said and sat down on the end of her bed, handing her mug over. 'Cheers.' He touched his mug against hers and grinned. 'It's a lovely spring morning out there,' he announced.

'Good.' Anna smiled again. 'Be just right for our planned drive over to Liverpool then.'

'Yep.' Mick nodded and took a sip of his tea. He looked at her, head on one side. 'Now, are you really sure you feel up to doing this? We can always do it another day if you still feel worried about going back to your folks' place.'

Anna shrugged. 'I'll be fine, I've got to face it sometime. They'll definitely both be at work today as usual and the sooner I get it over with, the better. Then I don't ever need to go back to my family home. The way I feel about them now, I never want to see my parents again.'

'Okay. If you're absolutely sure, then that's fine by me,' Mick said. 'Let's just hope they haven't changed the locks and your old key works,' he added.

'Hmm, well, there is that, but it's a chance I have to take, Mick. I can't see that they would do it, but you never know. I left my usual set on my dressing table as instructed by my mother, but I'd forgotten about the other set that were in my handbag, thankfully.' Today they were going to try to get all of her belongings from her old home. Mick had borrowed his friend's car for the day, so it was an ideal time.

Anna was pretty sure that her parents would be at work, her father at the bank in the city centre where he was the manager and her mother at the Picton Library, also close to the city centre. They would be out of the house until at least six o'clock tonight, so she and Mick had plenty of time. The list of things she wanted to collect was over on the chest of drawers and she had a pile of empty cardboard boxes to pack everything in that Mick and Pete had collected for her from various stores and shops around the area.

Mick said he had a big suitcase she could borrow to put her clothes in. Once she'd got something half decent to wear, she planned to look for a job to help pay her way and cover the rent on her room. Both Pete and Mick had helped her out for the last few weeks, since her escape act from the convalescent home. But she knew she couldn't rely on them forever – they had their own finances to think about.

Laura had lent her some money too, as she'd recently received the capital from the sale of her family home. She and Pete were planning to get married and start looking for a house of their own as soon as Laura had finished her college course in July. Anna had some savings in the same bank where her father worked. Once she'd found her bank book in her old bedroom, she intended to withdraw some money – making sure to choose a different branch to where he worked – and pay Laura back right away. After the challenges and grief the last twelve months had thrown at her, and even though she had only just turned seventeen, Anna felt mature, strong and adult enough now to take charge of her own life. Never again would she allow anyone to control her like her parents and those evil nuns had done.

She finished her tea and handed her empty mug to Mick. 'I'll just take a quick shower and then I'm ready to go,' she announced, slipping out of bed and pulling her dressing gown on.

Mick got to his feet and smiled. 'I'm just going to make some toast. Would you like a couple of slices?'

'Oh, yes please.' Anna smiled.

'It'll be ready and waiting in the kitchen for you when you're out of the shower.' He winked at her and left the room.

Anna hurried back to her bed-sitting room, dried her long auburn hair with Laura's borrowed drier and tied it up in a high ponytail. She pulled on a pair of denim jeans and a pale blue T-shirt, topped with a light wool sweater. Although the early April day was bright and sunny, it wasn't that warm yet and, if they went for a walk round the city after she'd got her stuff, the wind that blew up from the Mersey could be vicious.

Mick had said last night that he'd love to see the Cavern Club, where the Beatles used to play regularly before becoming really famous, and perhaps take a walk around the dockside to get some lunch. She'd told him there was a great chippy down there and his face had lit up. She was looking forward to spending the day in his company, just the two of them. Mick was one of the kindest young men she'd ever met and she always felt safe and comfortable around him.

After losing Tony so tragically, she'd never thought she'd ever meet anyone else who mattered to her again. She'd felt so dead inside and then losing her babies as well had almost killed every emotion within her. But recently she'd felt a spark of life and hope beginning to grow inside her again and it was a nice feeling. Like she was gradually awakening from a very long sleep and realising that life actually does go on.

She looked at her reflection in the dressing table mirror and smiled as she saw that a bit of colour had returned to her cheeks at last, instead of the sad and pale complexion that had been staring at her for far too long. She definitely looked healthier and more cared for since she'd been living here at the shared house. The dark circles beneath her eyes had all but vanished too.

In the kitchen a plate of toast waited for her on the table as promised and it was still warm, with the butter melting, just how she liked it. Mick must have timed toasting the bread after he'd heard her hairdryer stop. A small pot of marmalade stood by the plate and a knife lay beside it. Bless Mick, she thought as he came back into the kitchen with his jacket and car keys, he was so thoughtful.

'Do you want another quick brew before we go?' he asked. 'There's tea left in the pot and I stuck a cosy on it to keep it warm. My mother taught me well.' He grinned as she nodded.

'Sure, I'll just have half a mug to wash the toast down,' Anna said. 'Otherwise I'll need the lavvy halfway to Liverpool.' She laughed and spread marmalade onto her toast while Mick poured her half a mug of tea.

'I'm looking forward to this trip,' he said. 'You'll have to give me instructions to Woolton once we get off the main road, though. It's a shame the powers that be are still dragging their heels over building that new motorway road that was supposed to link Manchester to Liverpool by now. The drive would have been a doddle. Anyway, I've found an old road map.'

Anna nodded. 'I've only ever been brought over this way once in the car and that was to be dropped off at The Pines, but I do remember seeing the odd road sign. I'm sure we'll manage.' She finished her breakfast and went to get her jacket and handbag from the bedroom.

'Here we are,' Anna said as Mick drove down Menlove Avenue. 'Next left on to Yew Tree Road just before Calderstone Park and the house is halfway down. Just here.' She pointed to a large pre-war, semi-detached house on the left-hand side of the leafy road. 'All looks quiet,' she observed. 'Dad's car isn't on the drive and all the windows are closed, so that means Mum's definitely out or the bedroom windows would be open. She's a fresh air fiend even in the depths of winter. That's a good sign. Do you want to back the car onto the drive so we can easily load the boxes in the boot after I've filled them?'

Mick nodded. 'Sure. You go and check the door first to make sure it opens and then I'll manoeuvre the car on.'

Feeling nervous, Anna jumped out of the vehicle and hurried to the glossy red-painted front door, keys clutched tight in her sweating palm. The spotless white net curtains at the front bay window were still and not twitching, another good sign. She tried to tell herself she had a right to be here and that her mother clearly wasn't at home. Holding her breath, she pushed a Yale key into the lock, turned it and let out a big sigh of relief as the door creaked open. She hurried inside and took a quick look around to make sure the house was indeed empty. She turned round and through the open door stuck up her thumb at Mick, who smiled and reversed the car carefully onto the drive.

The two of them carried several empty cardboard boxes into the house and upstairs to Anna's bedroom, which overlooked the back garden with its carefully manicured lawn and cultured shrubbery.

She looked around the room and sighed. The pink-and-white-painted room was exactly as she'd left it, the striped curtains half-closed across the window, but the single divan bed was stripped of bedding, just a pale pink floral eiderdown remaining folded at the foot of the bed. No personal items were lying around, as Anna had taken her make-up and toiletries, her diary and the small framed photograph of her and Tony that she'd kept beside her bed to The Pines with her. She took her bank book from the bedside table drawer and pushed it into her handbag. A few books were sitting on a chest of drawers on the back wall and she packed them into one of the boxes that Mick had lifted onto the bed. A stack of single records was packed away carefully too.

'I presume you want the record player as well?' Mick asked. 'It'll look nice in your room at the house. Be just right sitting up on top of the chest of drawers.'

'Yes, please.' Anna nodded and he took her blue and grey Dansette record player downstairs to the car, calling out, 'I'll bring the case up from the back seat now.' He came back up with his suitcase and Anna took her clothes from the wardrobe and drawers and folded them all into the case. It didn't take too long and within half an hour they were ready to leave. Mick got out the list Anna had made and they ticked everything off and did a last look around.

'You okay?' Mick asked, putting an arm loosely round her shoulders as she stood in the middle of the room and took a last wistful look at the bedroom where she'd slept since the day she was born.

She nodded and leant into his side and he held her tighter. 'I think so,' she replied sadly. 'I can never forgive them for not standing by me and at a time when I needed them most. Why couldn't they see how broken and upset I was after Tony's death?'

Mick shook his head. 'I don't know, love. How any parent can turn their back on a child in their hour of need is beyond me. It's just plain evil to do what they did to you. I don't blame you for the way you feel about them.'

'Well, they'll never know where I am from now on – I won't be leaving a forwarding address or a phone number. I might write to them one day, but not until I feel that I'm really ready to tell them exactly what I think of them.'

Mick smiled. 'That's my girl! Let's finish loading the car and then we can pop over to Tony's parents to see how they're doing. At least they've stood by you and kept in touch each week to make sure you're okay.'

Anna nodded. 'Those two are more like parents to me than my own ever were. Then we can drive into the city, have a bite to eat and I'll show you the Cavern Club. Oh, and by the way, I forgot to say as we passed it, but John Lennon's home where he used to live with his Aunt Mimi is just round the corner from here, on Menlove Avenue. I'll point it out as we go back that way.'

'Oh, wow! Great,' Mick said. 'And don't forget, *I* was supposed to remind you to get your birth certificate. You'll need it for the future, to prove your age and for identification and what-have-you.'

'Good job *you've* got a good memory,' Anna said with a shake of her head. 'How did I leave that off the list? Right, I won't be a tick.' She hurried into her parents' large front bedroom with its boring dark-brown velvet curtains and matching drab brown candlewick bedspread. *It looks so dull in here*, she thought – even a brightly patterned cushion or two would have helped to lift it a little; but she supposed it suited their rather sombre personalities.

She opened the door of a tall dark-wood wardrobe that stood in an alcove one side of the chimney breast. Climbing up on her mother's dressing table stool, she reached up for a small suitcase off the shelf and, jumping down, placed it on the end of the double divan bed. The case wasn't locked and it didn't take her long to locate her birth certificate. It was in an envelope, which she put back before carefully tucking the certificate into her handbag. She shoved the case back onto the shelf, closed the wardrobe door and pushed the stool into place under the dressing table. She hurried back to Mick on the landing and closed her parents' bedroom door. 'Right, let's get out of this horrible place and go and see Dot and Frank.'

'Lead the way,' Mick said, following her down the stairs with the loaded suitcase.

'Now you promise to keep in touch and let us know what you're up to,' kindly Dot said, as Anna kissed her goodbye after they'd spent a pleasant hour with her. Frank was out at his bowling club and Dot said he'd be going for a pint afterwards at the pub with his friends. Dot said he was sad to miss her and sent his love.

'I promise to ring you every Saturday morning,' Anna said, hugging her once more. Mick shook Dot's hand and thanked her for the tea and cake she'd given them.

'You look after her, young man. She's been through far too much sorrow for a girl of her age,' Dot said. 'I was hoping you'd come back to live in Liverpool with us,' she directed at Anna, 'but I can see that it might not be the best plan at the moment. You need space between you and your parents while you pick up the threads of your life again.'

Anna nodded. 'You're right, I do. And at the moment I'm

best off in Manchester with my friends. But one day, who knows? I might feel ready to consider coming back to my home city to put down roots but a lot of water needs to flow under the bridge first before that can happen. We'll come and visit you when we can, I promise. We're going to have a wander around the city now so I can show Mick the Cavern Club and other things he wants to see.'

Dot smiled. 'Well, you two enjoy yourselves – and drive carefully, Mick.'

Mick stared up at the Cavern Club building on Matthews Street and shook his head. 'So, this is it? Doesn't look much from the outside, does it? But I guess it's kind of special to the groups who were discovered here. You know, we have a couple of great clubs in Manchester: the Oasis and the Twisted Wheel. I'll check out which group's playing this weekend and I'll take you to see them, if you like.'

Anna smiled and nodded. She *would* like. It seemed ages since she'd been taken out anywhere. 'I'd love that,' she said. 'I really feel ready to start enjoying myself again. My babies and Tony are never coming back. I'll always miss him, of course, he was my first love, but he wasn't the type of boy who would have wanted me to waste my life, moping around and being miserable.'

Mick took her hand and squeezed it tight. He smiled at her as he looked into her eyes. 'It's good to hear you say that,' he said softly. 'And I hope you'll let me help you to pick up the pieces.'

'You've already been doing that, Mick. I don't know what I would have done without you, and Laura and Pete, to support me. The three of you have saved my sanity and probably my life; I felt I had nothing left to live for. I could see no point in being here any more before I decided to escape the convalescent home.'

Mick pulled her close and hugged her. 'Then let's start as we mean to go on.'

'With lunch?' She laughed as his stomach growled right on cue. 'Okay, fish and chips down the docks then.'

'Am I that easy to read?' he teased, raising an eyebrow.

'Just a bit,' she said, laughing, and took his hand as she led the way.

TWENTY-FIVE

DIDSBURY, MANCHESTER

July 2015

Laura cleared the last of the weeds from the overgrown plot, carried them to a nearby waste basket and then took out the wet cloth she'd carried in a plastic carrier bag. She squirted the cloth with bleach cleaner and did the best she could to rub away the years of moss and grime from the small, white marble head-stone. It could really do with a professional clean but that was something she could organise in the future.

It was enough to know that she'd found her birth mother Katy's grave. And unbelievably, just across the tarmacked path was her dad's grave too. She thought of all the times she'd come here to put flowers on his grave, including most weekends before she was sent to The Pines. It was more often than Audrey ever did, she thought, despite her false act as the weeping and wailing widow in front of friends at Dad's funeral.

She'd had no clue her mother's headstone was hidden just opposite, behind the pile of weeds. *If only...* but it was too late now for that. From now on she would visit the pair of them whenever she was in Manchester. Pete had dropped her off;

she'd told him she wanted to do this on her own, so he'd popped to see an old work friend. Then they were going to meet at the coffee shop across the road and pick his mother Angie up from Wythenshawe and take her back to West Derby with them for a few days.

It had been easy enough to locate the grave once she had given her information to the person in the office. She traced a finger over the engraved angel and placed a kiss on her fingers and blew it at her mum's name and inscription. *Katy Sims, beloved wife of Jack and dearest mother of Laura. Aged twenty-one. Now sleeping peacefully with the angels.*

All this time, Laura thought, sadness and anger coursing through her, all this time and she hadn't known, thanks to Audrey. She gritted her teeth and pushed the angry feeling away. She would waste no more time on that woman again, not ever. She got to her feet and turned to blow one last kiss at her dad's grave, where she'd placed a bunch of brightly coloured mixed summer flowers earlier.

'See you both soon,' she whispered and turned to stroll down the path towards the exit gates. The day was hot and sunny and she enjoyed the warmth on her bare arms. Over breakfast that morning, Pete had suggested they have a holiday soon. They'd been so busy that year that they hadn't booked anything yet.

It was their forty-ninth wedding anniversary in September, so she'd suggested they wait until then as it would be a bit cheaper to fly anywhere when the school holidays would be over. They would probably end up going to Greece again as they usually did. Crete was always lovely, so maybe a trip there. Laura was also a bit concerned about being away at the moment as so much was happening with the Facebook group; more and more people were joining by the day since the *Granada Reports* spot, and most of the local papers had covered the item too.

PC Miles was in regular contact and had made an important discovery from the birth certificate copies that people had shared; each one was signed by the same registrar at Macclesfield District registry office. A loopy signature from a J.C. Braithwaite. After making enquiries, she had discovered that Mr Braithwaite had retired many years ago and had then passed away, and the entry numbers listed on the certificates had tallied correctly with the numbers and names recorded against them in the registry records. So it didn't seem that a correct birth certificate had ever been filed, only these faked ones.

As such, there was little the police could do, but they were pretty certain that all the certificate owners were genuinely members of the 'stolen babies club', as they'd come to be called. Inspector Jackson had told Pete and Laura that Braithwaite had most likely been on The Pines payroll and received illegal remuneration for his part in each of the crimes.

As Laura crossed the road to the coffee shop where Pete was meeting her, she so hoped they were getting closer to finding Paul. Her phone was ringing in her handbag and she delved in to pull it out. Rosie's name flashed on the screen. 'Hi, love,' she answered. 'What's up?'

'Are you still out in Manchester, Mum?' her daughter asked.

'I am, yes. I've just left the cemetery. I found Katy's grave, it's made me feel so emotional.'

'I'll bet it has. Bless her, poor Katy. Glad you found her, Mum. Anyway, listen. I think your friend Lydia has joined the Facebook group. She's looking for her son, who was born the same year as our Paul. Too much of a coincidence for it not to be the same Lydia you've talked about that used to send the secret letters to Dad and Mary.'

'Oh wow, that's wonderful! It will be our Lydia. There wasn't another that year. I'll look it up when I get in the coffee shop if I can get Wi-Fi up and running. If you don't see me posting anything, let her know you're my daughter and that I'll be in touch when I get home. Let's hope she contacts Barbara, if they're still in touch. It would be so nice to meet up with them again. Right, I'm here now, love, so I'll go and bag a table. I've got to text your dad when I'm inside and he'll join me. See you in a while with your Nana Angie in tow.'

Rosie laughed down the phone. 'Can't wait. She's such a character. Wonder what she'll be wearing today?'

'Jeans, knowing Angie, with her hair all colours of the rainbow. No old-lady stuff for your nana.' She said goodbye, then ordered a coffee and a blueberry muffin from the counter and took herself over to a table by the window. The young barista said he'd bring her order over in a moment. She sat down and sent a text to Pete.

She gazed out at the traffic passing by and tried to arrange her jumbled thoughts, wondering if Paul or any of his friends or family had seen the group yet, although there was no reason to think they would do. Paul may have no clue he had been adopted. He might not even be in the UK. She looked up and smiled at the young man who brought her order to the table.

He reminded her of Julian, her grandson, and she wondered if Paul might look anything like him; tall and dark-haired, probably more like Pete now, as their son was only eighteen years younger than his father. It was hard to think of him as a grown man. 'Thank you, that looks amazing.' She admired the artwork on her coffee; a long feather with intricate trailing detail. Clever.

Maybe the young man went to the Hollings, although, thinking about it, she didn't know if her old college was still open. She thought about Mary and wished they'd kept in touch more, but her friend was now married and had emigrated to Australia years ago. They emailed on birthdays and at Christmas, so it was better than nothing, but time was marching on and they were not getting any younger. She'd write to Mary tonight.

She looked up as the door opened and Pete strolled in. He

waved and smiled at her and went to the counter to place his order. Laura stared at his back and grinned, feeling a little thrill run down her spine. In spite of his silver hair – which she felt only added to his charms – he was still as slim and fanciable as the first time she'd met him when he'd held her in his arms at the youth club and they'd danced to the Ronettes. What a journey they'd been on and it wasn't quite over yet. She opened up her phone and started to type a message to Lydia.

Back in West Derby, Laura saw that her mother-in-law was sitting comfortably on the sofa with a mug of tea and went into the hall to call her daughters to let them know that Nana was in residence.

'What colour's her hair this time?' Penny asked, giggling.

'Pink and purple,' Laura whispered. 'It actually doesn't look too bad. It's styled in a nice bob, with stripes! See you soon.' She went back to join Angie, and Pete, who had just nearly put his back out, lugging Angie's case upstairs.

'Have you got a body in that case, Mother?' he'd joked as he limped into the lounge, holding his back. 'You're only here for three days.'

Angie laughed. 'You're a cheeky monkey, our Pete. You know I like to dress nice when we're having a bit of a family get-together. Well, I couldn't make me mind up, so I brought most of my wardrobe with me – I thought Laura could help me choose.'

* * *

Pete stood with his arm round Laura's shoulders as they watched their girls and their grandchildren fussing over Nana, who was in her element. You'd never guess she was in her late eighties; she still had bags of energy. Their youngest grandson Marcus was on her knee and she was talking to him about his latest Thomas the Tank Engine that he was clutching in his hands.

'Eeh, this takes me back,' Angie said, looking up at Pete with a smile. 'You used to be Thomas mad. All you boys did. You've a lovely family, you two,' she said proudly. 'In spite of your rocky start, you've done well. I just wish... well, you know what I just wish, don't you?' she finished, her voice filled with emotion.

'We do, Mum,' Pete said, giving Laura a squeeze. 'Keep your fingers crossed that something comes of this new Facebook group in the not-too-distant future.'

'Ah, Mum, Rosie and I have sent DNA samples to Ancestry.com today,' Penny announced. 'We just thought we should cover all avenues to see if we have any links out there. You never know.'

Laura smiled. 'Good luck. I suppose me and your dad should do that too.'

'Well yes, if you want to, but you'll get linked to us, obviously. Wait and see if ours unearth anything first and take it from there.'

After their family had left to go home and Pete had made sure his mum got upstairs safely, and announced he was jumping in the shower, Laura switched on her laptop, which was sitting on the dining table. She waited while it fired up and then logged into her Facebook account. She smiled when she saw that Anna was online and sent her a message. Anna responded immediately. *Can I call you? Something's happened.*

Of course, ring my mobile so we don't disturb Pete's mum, who's gone to bed, Laura sent back and went to get her phone from the coffee table in the lounge. She turned down the sound and within seconds, it vibrated. Laura answered. Anna's excited voice came down the line.

'You're not going to believe this, but I think I've found one of my daughters,' she gasped.

'What? Oh my God, that's amazing! But how do you know?'

'Look on the site for Abigail Porter,' Anna said. 'She joined the group earlier, but I know you've had a busy day today so thought I'd leave letting you know until tonight.'

Laura clicked on the profile of Abigail Porter and caught her breath. The woman was the living image of Anna a few years ago. Still like her now, in fact: thick auburn hair worn loose about her shoulders, blue eyes and Anna's smile. Laura's eyes filled with tears. There surely could be no mistake if looks were anything to go by.

'Are you looking?' Anna asked excitedly. 'What do you think?'

'I'm gobsmacked. She's your double.'

'Yes, she thinks so too,' Anna said. 'We've been messaging all evening and she's sent me images of when she was a teenager and a child and she is me through and through. She was adopted but only found out after her adoptive parents both died a few years ago. She's tried to find her roots but to no avail, until a friend told her about mother-and-baby search groups on Facebook and she found ours. My profile pic as admin was one of the first she saw and made her look twice.'

'Oh wow, Anna! Have you given her PC Miles's email?'

'Yes, and she's sending her a scanned copy of her birth certificate tonight. Her birth was registered at Macclesfield by J.C. Braithwaite, so it's looking like she's definitely one of mine. She had no idea about her sister but she told me that all her life she's felt like something, a part of her, was missing. We're going to get DNA tests done tomorrow and take it from there and then hopefully, we may find her sister.' Anna's voice wobbled with emotion as she continued. 'Oh, and, by the way, I have two grandchildren, one of each.'

'Oh, Anna, that's wonderful. I'm so happy for you. I can't wait to tell Pete. What does Mick say?'

'He's over the moon. Fingers crossed it all works out and Abigail and I are really mother and daughter. I know I have to be cautious and not put all my eggs in one clichéd basket, but I don't really have any doubts.'

TWENTY-SIX

DIDSBURY, MANCHESTER

August 1965

On the morning of the last Saturday in August, Mick dropped Laura and Anna at the dressmaker's in Didsbury village. Mick had offered them a lift as Pete was working that day. The pair got out of the car, buzzing with excitement. They said goodbye to Mick and before he drove away, Anna told him, 'We'll get the bus into Manchester from here and do some more shopping and then get the bus back. You don't need to pick us up – I've no idea how long we'll be.'

'Okay, that's fine,' he replied. 'I want to spend some time today getting this car cleaned and ready for our trip up to Scotland next week. Can't risk it breaking down, can we?' He grinned.

'Heaven forbid,' Laura said, laughing. She patted the bonnet of his new silver Ford Cortina fondly and Mick smiled proudly. 'Anyway, it's brand new so that's hardly likely to happen,' she finished.

'I know, but I want us to arrive in style, so I'll make sure it's well polished and freshly washed for you lovely ladies.' Mick had taken the plunge and bought the new car with financial help from his dad, who he was paying back in monthly instalments.

'We'll see you tonight,' Anna said, kissing him. 'Have fun polishing your bonnet.' She laughed as he hugged her tight. After less than a month of him taking her to see Geno Washington & the Ram Jam Band at the Twisted Wheel club in town, and on several subsequent dates, she and Mick had fallen in love and he'd asked her to marry him.

Anna had known that being with Mick forever was what she wanted from the first date and she'd had no hesitation in accepting his proposal. They both agreed there was no point in waiting until they were older. The following week the four of them were off to Gretna Green to be married over the blacksmith's anvil; a double wedding with no family interference and no parental permissions required.

Both couples had planned and booked their big day and accommodation, and now Laura and Anna were picking up their wedding outfits from the dressmaker and then popping into town for new shoes and handbags.

The two girls entered Madame Hettie's shop and the immaculately groomed assistant behind the counter greeted them with smiles and a friendly handshake. The name on the badge pinned to her smart beige two-piece suit was Sally. 'Please take a seat,' she said, pointing to two plush red velvet chairs next to a small mahogany occasional table. 'Madame Hettie won't be long; she's just upstairs with a client. Can I offer you ladies a cup of tea while you're waiting?'

Laura smiled and nodded. 'Thank you, that would be lovely.'

Within minutes, a silver tray complete with tea in rosebud-patterned china cups and saucers and shortbread fingers on a matching plate were placed on the small table beside them. 'Help yourselves to sugar,' Sally said, pointing to a small matching bowl and went back to stand behind the glass-topped counter, where she began cutting samples of lace fabric into squares and placing them in a neat pile.

Laura and Anna sipped their tea, glancing around the show-room area at mannequins dressed in fancy gowns, their wigged heads topped with long lace veils held in place by glittering tiaras or silk rosebud headdresses. Neither girl had chosen tradi-tional white gowns, as both had agreed it wouldn't feel right given their circumstances, and Laura had suggested they get married in something they could wear again rather than waste money. No one else knew about the planned wedding and that was the way they wanted to keep it for now. They'd agreed on maybe having a night out with all their friends at the youth club to celebrate eventually; something that would take very little planning and not cost them a lot. Pete and Mick would inform their parents when the foursome came home. For now, all they'd said was that they were going away for a few days.

As Laura stacked their used china on the tray a smartly dressed blonde woman in her early twenties came down the stairs, followed by Madame Hettie herself, who smiled and nodded in the girls' direction.

'Well, thank you so much,' the young woman said. 'I look forward to my first fitting.'

'I'll be in touch as soon as we are ready for you, Miss Henshaw,' Madam Hettie said and held the door open as her client left. She turned to Laura and Anna. 'Do you want to follow me, ladies?' She led the way upstairs and into a large room that was partially curtained off with blue-and-white-striped fabric.

Laura assumed the fitting rooms were behind the blue curtains, as directly opposite were floor-to-ceiling mirrors.

Two outfits were hanging from the picture rail on padded coat hangers and Madam Hettie gestured towards them with her hand. 'All ready and waiting for your final approval,' she said. 'Now yours is the green dress and jacket,' she went on, looking at Anna, and handed her the hanger and held back a curtain for Anna to slip behind. 'Let me know when you are ready to be zipped up.' She turned to Laura and handed her the other outfit. 'And the dark pink is for you.' She held back another curtain and Laura went inside the cubicle to try on her wedding outfit.

After Madame Hettie had zipped up the backs of their dresses and helped them on with the short boxy jackets, Laura and Anna stood in front of the large mirrors, turning this way and that. The outfits were identical apart from the colours. Both wore slim-fitting sleeveless minidresses with white Peter Pan collars. The jackets were edge-to-edge and collarless so that the dress collars could be worn outside the necks of the jackets if the girls chose to do so. Anna's dark-auburn hair hung down her back in a shiny wavy curtain, complementing the bright-green bouclé fabric of her outfit. Laura's dark hair was currently shoulder length with a thick dark fringe and flicked out at the ends in the same style ITV's *Ready Steady Go!* presenter Cathy McGowan wore. The dark-pink fabric suited her colouring and reflected the rosiness in her cheeks. Madame Hettie smiled as both girls oohed and aahed with delight.

'You both look fabulous,' she said. 'Those outfits are so trendy, you could wear them anywhere. Just wait there for a moment while I fetch something for you.'

She hurried down the stairs as Laura and Anna looked at one another, smiling happily. 'Don't think Mary Quant could have done a better job, do you?' Laura said. 'She's got them just like the sketch idea I gave her.'

'They're perfect,' Anna said, 'and they fit us so well too.' She smiled as Madame Hettie came back upstairs, carrying two white corsages of silk rosebuds and greenery, sparkly beads stitched on some of the petals. She pinned one on each jacket and stood back, nodding.

'Just the job,' she said. 'Nothing too heavy, just enough. Those are a complimentary gift from me to wish you both all the best. Now, if you're happy with the style and fit of your outfits, I'll get them boxed up for you while you get dressed. Just hand them out to me on the hangers when you're ready. And then you can join me downstairs in the showroom.'

On the bus into the city centre, their outfits in boxes in shiny red bags with Madame Hettie's name in gold letters emblazoned across the front, Anna and Laura discussed what they were going to buy when they reached Market Street. The Dolcis shoe shop was the first stop on their list. Madame Hettie had advised that white medium-heeled shoes would look nice, with a matching white bag, and be more comfortable on the day than stilettoes. Laura had thanked her for her suggestions and kind extra gift.

'I guess she wouldn't know that we Mod girls wouldn't be seen dead in stilettoes,' Laura said now they were out of earshot. 'We leave them to the rockers.'

Anna smiled. 'Well, if I were still Tony's girl, a rocker is what I would be. However, I'm Mick's girl now and copying and loving your Mod style.'

'And it suits you,' Laura said. 'We're all the same deep down, I guess, whatever title we choose to label ourselves with, but stilettoes – heaven forbid. Louis heels for me every time. Right, here we are,' she said as the bus pulled up at the junction of Market Street and Piccadilly Gardens. 'Let's get cracking and then we can go in Lewis's café for some lunch. I'm feeling quite peckish now.'

As they crossed over Market Street and walked past the offices of Laura's dad's solicitor, her thoughts turned to the news in the last letter she and Pete had received from him at the end of June. He'd informed them that he'd done all he could in trying to trace their son but had hit a brick wall as there was simply no trace of him at all, neither his birth or adoption had ever been legally registered. He had managed to get all of Laura's money back from the sale of her family home and that would now stand them in good stead for their future. Laura felt a moment of sadness wash over her as she thought of how wonderful it would have been to share their new home with their son. She and Pete were very happy and would soon be married. All she could do now was look forward rather than back and hope in time Paul would find *them*.

On Monday morning, the trip to Scotland took them a bit longer than expected due to roadworks and heavy traffic, even though they'd set off at the crack of dawn, or so it had felt to Laura. By two o'clock they were approaching the Gretna Green hotel and nervous butterflies were dancing in Laura's stomach. She was just hoping that all the registering they'd done and the information they'd been asked for over the phone last month was correct. Her birth certificate and Pete's were stashed away safely in her handbag and Anna had hers and Mick's in her handbag too.

The twenty-nine days' required registration period was up tomorrow and the weddings were booked for Wednesday afternoon at two. There was nothing else they'd been asked to bring with them, so she was keeping everything crossed. At least they had a bit of time to rest and take a stroll or two around the area. It would do the four of them good to relax after the mad rush of the previous month. It had been so hard not to tell her college friend Mary when she'd popped round to visit them the other night, but they'd all agreed the fewer people who knew about the wedding for now, the better. Once they were home again, they would let people know and celebrate properly.

. . .

Laura and Anna helped each other to get ready in one of the large hotel rooms they'd booked. Pete and Mick had been packed off to the other room with their suits and a promise that they wouldn't come in and peep. They would meet the boys downstairs near the anvil, where the marriage ceremonies would take place, just before the appointed time.

'Are we leaving our hair down or putting it up?' Anna asked, running her fingers through her freshly dried shiny locks.

'Whatever you'd like,' Laura said. 'I'm leaving mine loose, I'm not a lover of those pinned-up dos that a lot of brides wear. And I know Pete prefers my hair down.'

'Loose it is then,' Anna agreed. 'I don't like the pinned-up styles either.' She grinned, her eyes twinkling. 'Laura, I'm so happy. I never thought I would ever feel like this again. I owe it all to you three. What would I do without you?'

Laura gave Anna a hug. 'I feel the same. There's just one more thing I would give my right arm for at this moment and that's to find our Paul. But at least if and when we do, he'll have two parents to care for him.'

'You will one day, I'm sure.' Anna wiped away a tear.

Laura nodded. 'I hope so. Right, are we ready? Hope they've got our rings in their pockets.' The couples were being witnesses for each other; Pete had Anna's ring to hand to Mick and hopefully, Mick had Laura's.

As Laura and Anna walked arm in arm towards the black-smith's anvil, Laura nodded towards where their smart boys were waiting, their backs to the girls. Laura stuck two fingers in her mouth and wolf-whistled in their direction. They both turned at once and the looks of admiration and love on their faces were something that would stay with her forever. She had no doubts at all in that moment that she and Anna were doing the right thing in marrying Pete and Mick that day.

'Wow! You both look stunning,' Pete said as Mick nodded

his agreement, seemingly lost for words, his eyes moist as he took Anna's hand in his and kissed it.

The wedding ceremony itself took very little time, but they were the most precious minutes of her life, Anna thought, as Mick looked into her eyes and said his vows. She said hers and then he slid the gold band on her finger and kissed her as instructed. This was so much better than the big fancy wedding that she knew her mother would have loved for her if she'd married the 'right' man. This was perfect, and Mick was more than right.

As Pete and Laura took their places by the anvil, Anna felt tears running down her cheeks, watching her friends tie the knot. They had all been through so much in the last few years, pain and anguish that could have been avoided. But it had made them all stronger and able to fight for what they believed was right.

In the restaurant after their weddings, Pete got to his feet and raising a glass of champagne, he toasted them all: 'Here's to our beautiful wives and to the four of us and the future, and may it be better than the past. Happy Wedding Day to us all.'

July 2015

Laura answered the door to Anna and Mick and led them into the lounge and they flopped down on the sofa. They were waiting to be joined by Inspector Jackson and PC Miles, who were bringing new information with them. Pete was in the kitchen, making the usual brew for everyone, and Laura went to help him and carried plates of cake back into the lounge. The doorbell rang and she hurried to let in the visitors, who greeted her like old friends, which was what they were fast becoming.

She and Anna had kept their promise and had been in regular contact with Olive, keeping her up to date with what was happening. Anna and Abigail's DNA were a perfect match and an excited Anna was going to meet her daughter for the first time on Sunday afternoon at Abigail's Surrey home. She and Mick were travelling south by train, had booked a nearby hotel and were planning on making a little holiday of it.

After finishing his tea, Inspector Jackson undid the brief-case he'd carried in and lifted out a sheaf of papers. 'Well,' he began, 'we've had several possible matches with birth dates and certificates registered at Macclesfield from people who joined the Facebook group or saw the two of you on TV and responded to the email address that was given out. PC Miles here has been busy matching up where she can and we have encouraged possible matches to get DNA tests done.'

'Oh, that's very promising,' said Anna.

'Yes, but one thing we need you to do is try and persuade Olive to let us arrange testing for her, as we have a young lady who has come forward with a birth certificate. We believe the young lady may be Olive's granddaughter and her mother, Olive's daughter. They actually only live in Chester, so it will be wonderful for Olive if we can link them and reunite her with family.'

'Oh, that would be fabulous,' Laura exclaimed. 'She will be thrilled to know she has family. I'll speak to her later and tell her you will be calling her and explain why.'

'Thank you. We'll pick her up and take her home, of course, so she has nothing to worry about. But if you can explain how this DNA link works and then she won't think we're doing anything nasty to her. Her daughter has had hers done, so all we need now is Olive's.'

'So that's one of Anna's found,' Laura said, 'and possibly Olive's family too. We just need our Paul to be located now.'

Anna nodded. 'Abigail is trying to find her sister but thinks she may be abroad and has no idea she is adopted. It could take some time.'

Inspector Jackson smiled. 'Any of the kids who were adopted by Americans or Canadians or anywhere else in the world for that matter won't have a clue this is happening here, that's where worldwide DNA testing will come in handy.'

Laura sighed. 'I think that's what's happened to Paul, I just don't feel he's in this country.'

Pete patted her hand. 'Maybe our girls' DNA tests will bring some news soon.'

. . .

'We're on our way over,' Penny said as Laura answered her phone. 'Is Dad with you?'

'Yes,' Laura told her. 'He's in the garden. See you soon.' She hurried to join Pete, who was cutting the lawn at the back of the house. 'The girls are on their way over,' she announced.

'Oh, have they got some news?'

'Penny didn't say.' It was almost three weeks since the last visit from the police and, apart from Olive agreeing to a DNA test, things seemed to have gone a bit quiet. Anna had met her daughter and, from the pictures she'd sent to Laura the first night via her phone, there was no mistaking that they were mother and daughter. Anna's happy face spoke volumes. Laura was thrilled for her friend and hoped that her other girl could be traced eventually too.

Lydia had responded to Laura's recent message and, although there was no sign of Lydia's son yet, it was good to be back in contact with her old friend again.

Judging by Penny and Rosie's excited faces when she let her girls in, Laura knew they had something good to report. They bounced into the lounge and flung their arms round their dad, who gave them both a hug. 'Sit down, you two,' he said. 'You look like you're gonna burst.'

'Oh my God, you're not gonna believe what we have to tell you,' Rosie began.

'We've found him, we've found our Paul!' Penny shrieked excitedly.

'No!' Laura clapped her hands to her mouth. 'Really? You haven't?'

'We have, Mum,' Rosie reassured her. 'We really have found our brother.'

'Are you sure it's Paul?' Pete asked, frowning. 'You have to be careful with scammers, you know. Don't be handing money over, just in case.'

'It's definitely Paul, Dad, and he hasn't asked for any money,' Rosie said, laughing. 'We've seen photos of him as a child and an adult and he's the spit of you. We've seen his birth certificate that shows a Macclesfield registration by Braithwaite. And the birth date is correct. He was on the database for DNA as he's been trying to find family, but he had no idea about the Facebook group. When we told him, he went to look and joined up and saw the profile pics of you and Anna, and the photo you shared of you and Dad as teens. He can see himself in Dad. He knows he's adopted, but he only discovered that fact after the death of his parents, which was why he joined Ancestry to try and do a family tree. He discovered no trace of anyone else other than us two and we're a full match.'

'I see,' Laura said, her stomach looping all over the place. 'So where does he live now, where was he brought up?'

'He lives in Memphis, Tennessee, not far from Graceland, he said, where he was taken after his parents adopted him. They came to England to adopt children through what they were told was a good Catholic society, as did another couple who were their good friends. The other couple adopted a baby girl who was two weeks older than Paul. They were brought up nearby, same school and what-have-you, and they became really good friends. She moved away and got married and then divorced and came back to Memphis. Curiosity got the better of her too after her adoptive parents died and then she realised that her birth certificate had the same registration details as Paul's. She's called Shirley and she and our Paul are now an item, he said. He's called Matthew, by the way.'

Laura stared at Rosie, her mouth wide, and then shook her head. 'Have you got a photo of them on your phone?'

Rosie nodded and opened her phone to show her parents all the photos Matthew had shared with her. He was instantly recognisable and so was his partner, Shirley. 'Can you see what we see, Mum?'

Laura nodded while Pete gasped. 'Anna's missing daughter is Shirley. She's the image of Abigail and Anna,' he whispered, looking stunned.

'Yes, she is, and she's now done a DNA test too so Abigail and Anna will get pinged when the match comes through. But I don't think they'll need it, do you?'

Laura shook her head. 'I can't take all this in. Anna's baby and mine, brought up in the same town together like that. It's amazing. You couldn't write it, could you?'

'No, but if you think about it, the adopters were all wealthy people who may not have been accepted down the normal route for legal adoption; too old or from seedy but wealthy backgrounds. The nuns filled a loophole and sold stolen babies to order. Many ended up abroad. Matt – he goes by the name of Matt – can't believe you live in Liverpool now. It's a city he's always wanted to visit.'

Laura and Pete looked at each other, tears pouring down their cheeks, as Rosie quickly dialled a number on her phone. She spoke quietly, 'Morning, Matt. Would you like to talk to your mum and dad?' She handed the phone to a stunned Laura, who couldn't speak for crying.

EPILOGUE

WEST DERBY, LIVERPOOL

September 2015

Laura looked around the brightly decorated concert room at West Derby Conservative Club and felt a little thrill go through her. She couldn't wait to welcome the guests and show off her handsome son. Tonight was not a night she'd ever thought she'd experience in her life. A celebration to end all celebrations. Stolen babies and their parents, reunited at last. Her son, who she was getting used to calling Matt, and their daughters and grandchildren, cousin Fliss and Pete's mum were to be joined by Anna, Mick, Anna's daughters and her grandchildren and Tony's parents, who were beyond thrilled to have their precious granddaughters in their lives.

Also joining them were Olive and her newfound family and the police inspector and PC who had helped to make this reunion a possibility. Lydia had sent them a good luck card but was unable to join them, although she said she hoped to catch up soon. She was still seeking her missing son. Pete's mum Angie, looking as colourful as ever, was helping with the children and in her element now her only grandson was back in the fold of his family, where he belonged.

Matt and Shirley had arrived the previous week and it had become apparent to Laura that the pair were very much in love. They told both couples that they wanted to live in the UK with their newfound families and had set the ball rolling to emigrate.

They had British birth certificates and planned to seek the advice of Fliss, Laura's cousin, to see how easy it would be to move to Liverpool. They would first need to go back to the US to put their family homes up for sale, but they had spent this week making plans. Laura and Pete were thrilled that the boy they'd waited forever to have back in their lives had made that decision almost right away after setting foot on UK soil.

Matt was a chef by trade and said he would love to open an American diner down near the docks, an area that he'd immediately fallen in love with. Pete had taken him for a wander around every day, looking at suitable properties and picking up the details in estate agents' offices to take home and study.

He'd loved hearing tales about his late grandfather Jack; the sad tale of his grandmother Katy had upset him and he had promised to go with Laura to visit both their graves before he went back to America. Hearing how both Laura and Anna had been packed off to The Pines angered him, but he agreed it was a sign of the times and America was pretty much the same in the way they dealt with pregnancies out of wedlock. He and Pete talked non-stop about UK football, which Matt had followed for years and agreed was better than American football, which they called 'soccer' in the US, and Pete was taking him to see an Everton match the following week.

As the room began to fill with friends and family, the DJ played some background music. Pete came to stand by Laura's side. He nodded in the direction of Matt and Shirley, who had taken to the floor for a little waltz around the room. 'It's so good to see those two together after all the years of not knowing what had happened to them.'

Laura nodded. 'Anna and I think so too. And we'll be related as soon as they get married, all one big happy family. Ah look, there's Olive and her family. Oh, look at her, bless, she looks lovely and she's glowing. Let's go and say hello.'

Olive proudly introduced her lovely family to Laura and Pete. 'I have so much to thank you for, my love,' she said to Laura. 'I actually belong to someone at last.' Her granddaughter Sally pulled her into her arms and smiled.

'And I've got a real nan at last,' she said. 'Thank you, Laura, for looking after her when you were a youngster yourself. And we're all so glad you've got your son back in your lives.'

By the end of the evening, when everyone had been introduced to everyone else and the buffet had been eaten and Laura was almost hoarse, she turned to PC Lucy Miles and gave her a hug. 'Thank you so much for all your help. You've made more than a few dreams come true.'

'It's been our pleasure, believe me.' She tapped the inspector on the arm. 'Phil, can we tell them our news now?'

Inspector Jackson smiled. 'I think we should. And call me Phil, by the way. It's been a pleasure working on this case and a great outcome so far. Let's just hope we can reunite more families soon.'

Lucy held out her hand to show off a solitaire diamond ring. 'We're engaged,' she announced gleefully. 'That's what happens when you're on a case for a long time,' she joked, smiling at Phil.

'Oh, congratulations, that's just perfect,' Laura exclaimed. 'I hope you'll both be very happy. Let's get the DJ to play mine and Pete's tune and we can all have a dance to it to celebrate.'

She dashed across the room to speak to the DJ and, as the opening chords of the Ronettes' 'Be My Baby' played, Pete took her in his arms and held her tight. He whispered in her ear, 'Back to where we started, my love, and boy, what a ride it's been! I love you more now than I ever did, if that's possible. And look...' He nodded his head in the direction of their son and Anna's daughter, who were dancing close by in one another's arms. 'I think the best is yet to come.'

A LETTER FROM PAM

Dear reader,

I want to say a huge thank you for choosing to read *A Child for Sale*. If you did enjoy it, and want to keep up to date with all my latest releases, just sign up at the following link. Your email address will never be shared and you can unsubscribe at any time.

www.bookouture.com/pam-howes

To my loyal band of regular readers, who bought and reviewed all my previous stories, thank you for waiting patiently for another book. Your support is most welcome and very much appreciated.

As always, a big thank you to Beverley Ann Hopper and Sandra Blower and the members of their Facebook group, Book Lovers. Thanks for all the support you show me. Also, thank you to Deryl Easton and the supportive members of her Facebook group, Gangland Governors/NotRights.

A huge thank you to team Bookouture, especially my lovely editor Maisie Lawrence – as always, it's been such a pleasure to work with you again – and also thanks to Jacqui Lewis and Jane Donovan for the copy-edit and proofreading side of life.

And last, but definitely not least, thank you to our amazing media team, Kim Nash, Sarah Hardy, Jess Readett and Noelle Holton, for everything you do for us. You're 'Simply the Best', as

Tina would say! And thanks also to the gang in the Bookouture Authors' Lounge for always being there. As always, I'm so proud to be one of you.

I hope you loved *A Child for Sale* and if you did, I would be very grateful if you could write a review. I'd love to hear what you think and it makes such a difference in helping new readers to discover one of my books for the first time.

I love hearing from my readers – you can get in touch on my Facebook page or through Twitter.

Thanks,

Pam Howes

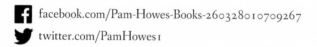

facebook.com/Pam-Howes-Books-260328010709267

twitter.com/PamHowes1

ACKNOWLEDGEMENTS

For my lovely and supportive partner, my gorgeous girls, my assorted grandchildren and my two new great-granddaughters; their wives, husbands and partners, and the rest of my family, as always. Thanks as always for all your support and love over the last few months. A big shout-out and thanks to the old sixties gang of recycled teens in the Manor Lounge FB group for being there with your treasured memories of those special days we all shared. Thanks also to my dear friends Brenda Thomasson and Sue Hulme for beta-reading. And a mention for my best writing buddy, my little pug Lennon, who never leaves my side while I'm working. Much appreciated as always. Lots of love to you all. Pam xxx

Manufactured by Amazon.ca
Bolton, ON

38850099R00129